The Suspect in the Smoke

"We just came from your house," Nancy told Mary McGregor, "and it has been broken into." Nancy saw Mary's eyes open wide. "We were afraid you might have been hurt, so we looked inside."

"It's pretty messed up," Bess added.

"It must have been a burglar," Mary said shakily.

"I don't think so," Nancy said. "While searching for you, we saw that several valuables were left untouched. Could someone be trying to scare you?"

Just then, Bess's mouth dropped open. "Oh, no!" she gasped, pointing toward the street.

Nancy looked out the large window at the front of the house. Her heart jumped as she saw a billowing cloud of black smoke. Growing bigger and thicker, it completely engulfed Mary McGregor's car!

Nancy Drew
Mystery Stories

Available from MINSTREL Books

115

NANCY DREW®

THE SUSPECT IN
THE SMOKE

CAROLYN KEENE

A
MINSTREL®
BOOK

PUBLISHED BY POCKET BOOKS

New York   London   Toronto   Sydney   Tokyo   Singapore

This book is a work of fiction. Names, characters, places, and incidents are either products of the author's imagination or are used fictitiously. Any resemblance to actual events or locales or persons, living or dead, is entirely coincidental.

A MINSTREL PAPERBACK *ORIGINAL*

A Minstrel Book published by
POCKET BOOKS, a division of Simon & Schuster Inc.
1230 Avenue of the Americas, New York, NY 10020

Copyright © 1993 by Simon & Schuster Inc.
Produced by Mega-Books of New York Inc.

ISBN: 0-671-79301-2

First Minstrel Books printing October 1993

10 9 8 7 6 5 4 3 2

NANCY DREW, NANCY DREW MYSTERY STORIES, A MINSTREL BOOK and colophon are registered trademarks of Simon & Schuster Inc.

Cover art by Aleta Jenks

Printed in the U.S.A.

Contents

1

A Recycled Warning

"Watch out!" Nancy Drew shouted over the roar of machinery. She grabbed Bess Marvin's shoulder and pulled her sideways just as a forklift whizzed past, close to where her friend had been standing.

"Hey, be careful!" Bess yelled at the driver, whipping her long blond hair around as she turned. The forklift quickly disappeared behind a stack of large wooden bins at the River Heights recycling center. Bess turned to Nancy and said, "He almost hit me." Her blue eyes sparkled with anger.

"I guess we'd better be alert," Nancy said, shaking back her shoulder-length, reddish-blond hair. The driver should slow down for safety's sake, Nancy knew. Still, she was glad to see so much activity at the center.

The large blacktop lot was dotted with crushing and baling equipment. To Nancy's right, two girls threw aluminum cans into the mouth of a cartoon-style alligator. The cans traveled up a conveyor belt and into a large crusher.

To Nancy's left, three strong boys took turns pushing wheeled carts full of recyclables onto a large scale and writing down the weight of each cartload.

The whole area was surrounded by a chain-link fence. Along the fence were stacked all sorts of bales, bins, and barrels of paper, cardboard, aluminum, crushed glass, and other recyclables.

"I guess buying and selling people's garbage is big business," Bess said, looking around at the high walls of stacked cardboard and paper.

"It sure is," Nancy agreed. "And for the next week most of the profits will be donated to the River Street Recreation Center."

"I sure hope we can raise enough money to rebuild the rec center." Bess sighed. "I really miss my aerobics class there. It's been three weeks since I've exercised, and my hips look bigger already."

Three weeks ago a fire had destroyed the gym and several offices at the River Street Recreation Center, a popular spot in River Heights. Many people, from young kids to senior citizens, depended on the center as a place for basketball and volleyball games, karate and gymnastics lessons, crafts workshops and social events.

Many of the townspeople were pitching in to help raise funds to rebuild the burned portion of the center. Over the next week they hoped to raise ten thousand dollars. That would be enough to pay for designing a new building. Once that was done the River Street center board of directors hoped to get a special grant for the actual building.

Nancy had volunteered to coordinate several events run by the young kids and teenagers. She had worked especially hard to get publicity and volunteers for this first weekend. She knew that without a good kickoff weekend the week-long fund-raising drive would almost certainly fizzle. From what Nancy could see, this first event, at least, was going to be a success.

"Let's find George so we can get out of here," Bess said, letting Nancy lead the way across the lot.

Bess's cousin, George Fayne, was in charge of the recycling project. She kept track of the amounts of recyclables River Heights citizens were donating. Teen volunteers were collecting bottles, cans, papers, and magazines from all over town. Once the center had sold the recycled

3

material, the money would go into the rebuilding fund.

This was just the first day of a busy week for the youths of River Heights. A car wash would begin on Tuesday, run by a group of boys and girls who called themselves the Car Wash Kids. On Wednesday evening a karaoke machine would be set up at the rec center, in a part of the building that was undamaged by the fire. The karaoke machine played music to popular songs while showing the words on a screen. Kids could make a donation to sing their favorite songs into a microphone on stage.

Senior citizens were also heavily involved in the fund-raising drive. They needed the River Street center for social events, crafts workshops, and exercise classes. Led by a woman named Mary McGregor, the senior citizens were running a five-day crafts bazaar and a big fund-raising dinner on Saturday night.

"I bet we're earning a lot of money here this weekend," Bess said.

As treasurer for the youth activities, Bess had to keep track of the money raised at each event. Bess also had the job of painting a ten-foot-tall thermometer on a sign at the front of the rec center. Instead of degrees the thermometer was marked off in various dollar amounts up to ten

4

thousand dollars. A red line on the sign would show how much money had been raised so far.

"Nancy, Bess, over here!"

The girls turned to see George wave eagerly to them. She was holding a clipboard and talking to a dark-haired man in coveralls. At five foot eight, George was almost as tall as the man. Nancy could see her brown eyes sparkle as she and Bess approached. George's short, curly brown hair was neat, even in the hubbub of the recycling center.

Neither George nor the man seemed to notice the huge conveyor belt that hummed behind them. Almost eight feet off the ground, it carried cardboard in pieces of every size and shape to a huge crusher. Once flattened, the cardboard was stacked and tied into four-foot-tall bales.

"That must be the world's largest garbage compactor," Bess said as a forklift hauled away one of the large bundles.

"Each bale of cardboard weighs about a ton," George replied. "They are sold to a company that makes new boxes."

"Oooh, no," groaned Bess, turning to Nancy. "Let's get her out of here before she becomes more of an expert on garbage."

"Recyclables, not garbage," George corrected with a smile. "And I can't leave for at least

5

another hour. We've had so much stuff turned in that we haven't been able to keep up. Maybe you two could help."

Bess groaned again as George pointed toward a large pile of mixed recyclables.

"That stuff got mixed up when some bins tipped over," George said. "We need to separate the magazines and newspaper."

Nancy and Bess went to work on the pile. Following George's instructions, Bess started pulling magazines from the mess and tossing them in a wooden bin on her left. Nancy concentrated on the newspaper, tossing it into a separate bin.

After half an hour Nancy's back was starting to ache from bending over the pile. She was glad to see George walk over.

"I see Bess is reading on the job," George joked as she nudged her cousin. Bess was leaning against the wooden bin, flipping through a copy of *Healthful Eating* magazine that she had pulled from the pile.

"I'm just taking a short break," Bess protested, looking up from her magazine. Then, adding a businesslike tone to her voice, she said, "And waiting for your financial report. I hope it's ready, Ms. Fayne."

George laughed and answered brightly, "We've earned four hundred dollars for the rec center. I just talked to the manager, and he has recorded almost eight hundred pounds of aluminum cans and nearly ten tons of cardboard and paper turned in so far."

"More than ten tons of garbage, and we've only earned four hundred dollars?" Bess said in disbelief. She rolled her blue eyes.

"It's not garbage," George corrected again. "And besides, when you put it with the money earned from the other fund-raisers, it will all add up."

Leaning against her bin of newspapers, Nancy caught sight of a headline on one of the discarded papers. "'River Street Recreation Center Up in Smoke,'" she read aloud.

The front page of the three-week-old paper was devoted completely to the spectacular fire. At the top a huge picture showed the building with flames shooting out of the gymnasium windows.

"It's hard to believe all that damage happened because someone left papers too close to a space heater," George said, looking over Nancy's shoulder. "Do you think it was Mrs. McGregor who was so careless? The fire did start in her office, after all."

"Mrs. McG said she didn't put the papers there, and her word is good enough for me," Bess said firmly. Like a lot of other young people who used the center, Bess had gotten to know the older woman well and was very fond of her.

"I agree, it's not like Mrs. McG to be so careless," Nancy said. "Someone else could have left the papers there and been afraid to admit it. Her office is never locked, you know."

Nancy liked Mrs. McGregor, too. The energetic volunteer had made the rec center an important part of her life since the death of her husband seven years ago. She seemed always to be teaching a class or solving some problem. She spent so much time there, she had even been given an office.

The mayor had appointed five civic leaders to a board of directors to oversee major decisions at the rec center, and a friendly secretary took care of the bookkeeping. But to most people, Mrs. McGregor was the heart and soul of the center.

George reached over Nancy's shoulder and pointed to a second picture on the newspaper's front page. It was a head-and-shoulders shot of a middle-aged man in a T-shirt. Beside it was a third photo of a slim woman in an attractive business suit talking to fire fighters.

"I hope they can find that manager—Nikos Manolotos," George said, reading the name under the man's picture.

"Is he the one who stole the money that was

supposed to pay for the insurance?" Bess asked, looking up from her magazine.

"The police haven't charged him with a crime," Nancy said, looking at Nikos's picture. "But it was his job to send the money to Safeguard Insurance each month. The Safeguard people say they never received the money."

"If those payments had been made, there would have been insurance money to rebuild the rec center," George fumed. "I sure would like to know where that Manolotos guy is."

"So would the police, but he disappeared right after the fire," Nancy said, handing the newspaper to George.

George looked again at the third photo on the page. "That Stephanie Mann certainly manages to get her picture in the paper a lot," she said.

"Being chairwoman of the rec center board of directors has gotten her a lot of publicity," Nancy agreed, pulling the last few newspapers from the pile.

Then the three girls were startled by an unusually large crunch from the cardboard baling machine. "That machine gives me the willies," Bess said with a shiver.

The girls scooted quickly out of the way as a forklift fitted with a small plow darted toward them. The operator gave them a quick thumbs-up signal, and the forklift pushed the pile of cardboard they had just finished sorting toward the compactor.

"Oooooh, dear!" Bess cried suddenly, holding up a small slip of yellow paper. "I think someone's in trouble." She handed the paper to Nancy.

A brief message was printed in stiff, all-capital letters.

" 'KEEP YOUR NOSE WHERE IT BELONGS OR YOU MAY BE IN GRAVE DANGER,' " Nancy read out loud.

"It was in this magazine," Bess said, holding out the copy of *Healthful Eating*.

Nancy took the magazine and turned it over. She stared at the address label. The magazine was addressed to Mary McGregor!

2

Search for a Friend

"Are you sure the note came from here?" Nancy asked, flipping through the magazine.

"Positive!" Bess insisted, raising her hands. "I saw it fall out of that magazine."

"But who would threaten Mrs. McGregor?" George asked. "She's the most popular volunteer at the rec center."

"We don't even know for sure that this note was sent to Mrs. McG," Nancy said. "It might have been pushed into her magazine while all those recyclables were being moved around."

"But what if someone *is* threatening Mrs. McG?" Bess insisted. "We've got to see if she needs help. Her house is on the way to mine. We should at least stop there and see if she's home."

Nancy agreed. George went off to tell the

recycling center manager that she was leaving for the day. When she returned the three girls walked to Nancy's blue sports car. Nancy had tucked the threatening note in her pocket. Bess still carried the *Healthful Eating* magazine under her arm.

The cool autumn breeze felt good through the open car windows. Nancy drove slowly as they reached River Heights's east side.

"Mrs. McG's house is just around this corner," Bess pointed out. "I remember because I gave her a ride home from the rec center once."

Nancy stopped her car in front of a small white house with attractive peach-colored trim. Carefully pruned rose bushes lined both sides of the walk.

"I hope we don't bother her with our questions," George said as they walked to the house. "I'm starting to feel silly suspecting that anyone would threaten Mrs. McG."

"I know what you mean," Nancy said.

Bess rang the doorbell.

As they waited for an answer Nancy noticed that the wood in the door frame was splintered and the latch was broken, as though someone had kicked in the door.

Nancy looked at her friends. George and Bess had seen the broken latch, too.

"It looks like someone broke in," Bess whispered. She glanced fearfully toward the two corners of the house. "What if there's a burglar inside?"

Nancy leaned close to the door and listened. There was no sound. "There's only one way to find out," she whispered. Then she gave the door a gentle push. It swung open with a soft creak. Nancy poked her head around the door and into the small living room.

Bess threw her hands up. "Who could have done this?" she gasped.

To the left of the door Nancy saw an over-turned table and a shattered vase. Roses lay crushed and broken on the hardwood floor. Framed pictures that had hung on the wall were on the floor. An overstuffed chair was tipped on its side, and the television set had been thrown off its stand.

"What if Mrs. McG is in there hurt?" Bess said, stepping back from the doorway.

"We'd better find out," Nancy answered, quietly edging her way into the house. She stood still and listened intently.

"Bess, you stay here and get help if there's trouble," Nancy said. She motioned for George to check the kitchen, which lay to the right through a small arch.

Nancy stepped over the trampled flowers and walked cautiously toward the bedroom door, to

13

the left of the living room. From the doorway she could see a jewelry box had been emptied onto the bed and then tossed aside. Dresser drawers were pulled open. Shirts and nightgowns were flung on the floor. On top of the dresser a dollar bill and some change remained untouched.

Nancy's heart pounded as she opened the closet door, but there was no sign of Mary McGregor or the criminals.

Down the hall bath powder had been dumped on the bathroom floor, and blue shampoo had been squirted on the mirror.

"I didn't see anyone," Nancy said when she joined George and Bess at the front door. "I don't think this was done by a thief. Money and jewelry were left in the bedroom, and the TV is still here."

"And there are silver candle holders on the dining room table," George said. "But the kitchen's a mess—someone dumped flour and sugar all over the floor."

"Thank goodness Mrs. McG wasn't here," Bess said, shaking her head.

"What if she *was* here—and was kidnapped?" George suggested, throwing a worried glance around the ransacked house.

"We'd better call the police," Nancy said. Scanning the room, she spotted the telephone. It had been knocked on the floor but was still connected. She lifted the receiver and dialed the police. After giving the dispatcher the address of Mrs. McGregor's house and some brief details, Nancy hung up.

Next Nancy dialed the River Street center. The secretary, Sammie Sanders, told her that Mrs. McGregor had left shortly after lunch and hadn't been seen since.

Nancy rejoined George and Bess on the front steps, pulling the door shut behind her. The three girls moved uneasily down the front walk.

At the sidewalk Nancy stopped to peer up and down the quiet street. There were a few cars parked in driveways, and several houses away a woman was raking up the first fallen leaves.

"Let's split up and see if the neighbors saw anything suspicious," Nancy suggested.

"Good idea. I'll go left and check the next few houses," George offered.

"Then I guess I'll go to the right," Bess said, turning toward a two-story brick house on the other side of Mrs. McGregor's. There was a large German shepherd chained near the door.

Bess took a deep breath, and Nancy heard her say, "I'll even face that dog if that will help us find Mrs. McG." Nancy smiled as she watched Bess lengthen her strides and head down the sidewalk. "Go for it, Bess!" Nancy called out.

Nancy crossed the street and began knocking

on doors. She got no answer at the first three houses. She could see that her friends were having no better luck on their side of the street. Was the whole neighborhood deserted?

Perplexed, Nancy walked up the steps of a blue house with yellow chrysanthemums blooming in front. She raised her hand, but before she could knock the door flew open.

A small, elderly woman in a flowered cotton dress gasped in surprise. "Why, good morning," the woman stammered. "I was just going out for a walk, and . . . there you were!"

"I'm sorry I startled you. I'm Nan—"

"Nancy Drew," the woman finished with a smile. "I've seen your picture in the newspaper with stories about the crimes you've solved. You're the famous teen detective! Mary McGregor told me you were working on the River Street rec center fund-raising drive with her."

"Yes, I am." Nancy nodded, hoping that this observant woman would have noticed something useful.

"I'm Thelma Williams," the woman said. "Won't you come in?"

Nancy hesitated. She didn't want to offend her best hope for information, but if Mrs. McGregor was in trouble, time was important.

"I'm sorry, I can't," Nancy said. "I'm looking

16

for Mrs. McGregor. She left the rec center just after lunch. Do you know where she might be?"

"Perhaps she's with Horace," Mrs. Williams said. "Horace Bell. He lives just a few blocks from here. Maybe he's cooking dinner for her, since her plumbing is out of order."

"Her plumbing is out of order?" Nancy asked alertly. "Did she tell you that?"

"Why, no, but the plumbing truck was there this morning," Mrs. Williams said. "About ten o'clock, I think. It didn't stay long. I thought the plumbers might come back with more parts or something. But they never did."

"What company?" Nancy asked, hoping Mrs. Williams would remember.

The woman raised her eyebrows and touched her fingers to her chin. "There wasn't a company name on the van," she finally answered. "It just said 'Plumbing' on the side in white letters. It showed up well against the dark gray."

"You said Horace Bell lives near here. Do you know his address?" Nancy asked, reaching in her pocket for a notepad and pencil.

"I don't know the house number, but it's on Cottage Place," Mrs. Williams said. "I pass there on my walks."

Nancy jotted down Horace Bell's name and the street while Mrs. Williams locked her door.

The friendly older woman walked with Nancy to the sidewalk, then waved and headed off on her afternoon stroll.

Nancy crossed to her car, where Bess and George were already waiting.

"I found out that Mrs. McGregor drives a maroon four-door car," George said as Nancy approached. "That's all I learned."

"And I struck out completely," Bess said with a sigh. "I faced that giant dog for nothing. How about you?"

Nancy told her friends about her conversation with Thelma Williams.

"Do you think someone in a plumbing van could have kidnapped Mrs. McG?" Bess asked Nancy.

"Possibly, but let's hope she's just visiting her friend Horace," Nancy said. "We can check the phone book for his address."

Nancy led the way back to Mrs. McGregor's house. While Bess and George waited outside for the police Nancy found Horace's name among a long list of Bells in the phone book. She dialed the number but got only a busy signal.

Nancy just had time to jot down the number and the address—1411 Cottage Place—before a police car pulled up to the curb.

Bess and George were talking to the young

18

policewoman, Sergeant Benson, when Nancy joined them. Nancy added her information about the plumbing van. She showed the policewoman the damaged door and then left, promising to call the police station if she learned any more about Mrs. McGregor's whereabouts.

The girls jumped into Nancy's car and were soon cruising down Cottage Place.

"Fourteen-oh-seven, fourteen-oh-nine," Bess counted down as Nancy slowed the car. "There, the yellow house with the white trim."

"And there's a maroon four-door out front," George said. "We're in luck."

Nancy parked the car, and the anxious girls hurried up the walk. Nancy pushed the doorbell and immediately heard a dog barking and a man's voice. "Quiet, Flip," the man said. The dog was instantly silent, and the door opened.

Nancy smiled at the slender, bald man standing in the doorway. A small brown-and-white dog stood obediently beside him. The hair on the dog's neck bristled, but he didn't bark again.

"I'm Nancy Drew," Nancy started. "I'm looking for Mary McGregor."

Mr. Bell gave Nancy, Bess, and George a stern look.

"What do you want with her?" he challenged. "If this has anything to do with—"

"Oh, Horace." A curt voice behind him cut him off. "Stop being so protective. This is my youth coordinator." Mary McGregor stepped into the doorway, her gray eyes sparkling.

"And Bess and George," she added, putting a friendly hand on each cousin's shoulder.

"Do come in," Mrs. McGregor said. "And don't worry about the dog—Flip won't bite."

Mr. Bell held the door open reluctantly. "What can I do for you girls?" Mrs. McGregor asked when they were all inside the small living room.

Nancy, George, and Bess looked at one another. They were relieved that Mrs. McGregor was safe, but now they had to tell her about her house. Finally Bess held out the threatening note.

"I was sorting stuff at the recycling center," Bess said, "and I found this in one of your magazines."

"Oh, that silly thing," Mrs. McGregor said as she glanced at the note. "Probably from one of the kids at the rec center, angry with me for making him clean up his spilled pop or something like that. I don't have time for such nonsense."

"The note was written to you?" George asked.

"Well, yes. I found it slipped under my door one morning," Mrs. McGregor said casually. "I just used it to mark my place in my magazine. It's hardly worth worrying about."

"I think maybe it is," Nancy said carefully.

"We just came from your house, and it has been broken into."

Nancy saw Mary's eyes open wide. Horace Bell clutched Mary's arm.

"The latch on the door was broken," Nancy said. "We were afraid you might have been hurt, so we looked inside."

"It's pretty messed up," Bess added. "Someone turned the furniture over and threw food around the kitchen."

Nancy glanced at Horace. His face was white, and he had slumped weakly into a chair. The dog sat quietly at his feet.

"It must have been a burglar," Mrs. McGregor said shakily.

"I don't think so," Nancy said. "While searching for you through the house we saw that several valuables were left untouched. Could someone be trying to scare you?" Nancy watched carefully for a reaction.

"Manolotos," Horace said, pushing himself to his feet. "I told you he was dangerous, Mary."

Nancy immediately recognized the name of the former building manager of the rec center.

"You think Nikos did this?" Nancy asked. "Why would he ransack Mrs. McGregor's house?"

Mr. Bell seemed flustered. "Mary won't leave him alone," he said. "Just last night there was

21

another story in the newspaper about her telling the police to work harder to find him. I told her not to do that."

"That's silly," Mary McGregor scolded him. "You have no reason to think Nikos was at my house. Even if he was, it doesn't matter. I won't be frightened by a few threats. I will continue to push for that man to be found and tried."

Just then Bess's mouth dropped open. "Oh, no!" she gasped, pointing toward the street.

Nancy followed Bess's gaze out the large window at the front of the house. Her heart jumped as she saw a billowing cloud of black smoke. Growing bigger and thicker, it completely engulfed Mrs. McGregor's car!

3

Trouble on Wheels

Nancy was two steps ahead of the others as she dashed out the front door and into the yard. The dog shot between Nancy's legs and barked several times before stopping on the lawn and waiting for Mr. Bell to catch up. Just then Nancy saw a boy whiz by on a skateboard. He was going so fast she couldn't get a good look at him.

Black smoke continued to roll up around the hood of Mrs. McGregor's car. Nancy looked around, wondering if Mr. Bell might have a fire extinguisher stashed somewhere. Before she could ask, Mrs. McGregor rushed out of the garage with a fire extinguisher in her hand.

"Thank goodness Horace is always prepared," she said, jogging toward the car.

Out of the corner of her eye Nancy saw Mr. Bell move toward Mrs. McGregor. "I'll take that," he said firmly, reaching for the extinguisher.

For a split second Nancy thought Mrs. McGregor was going to object. Instead the woman handed the extinguisher over to Mr. Bell, who walked quickly toward the street.

He sprayed the front of the car with foam and then popped the hood open and sprayed the engine. Flip followed close behind his master, his hair bristling and teeth showing. Mary and the girls stood back from the noxious fumes.

"What was that?" Bess asked breathlessly when the smoke had cleared.

"I didn't see any flames," Nancy observed. "I'd guess it was a smoke bomb."

Nancy stepped to the edge of the street and scanned the neighborhood in both directions, hoping to see whoever had set the bomb.

Everything looked the same as when they had arrived except that a small crowd of people had begun to gather across the street. Nancy saw Thelma Williams half walking, half running down the sidewalk.

"The police will be here in a moment," she yelled as she hurried to Mrs. McGregor's side. "I was on my daily walk when I saw the smoke. I went straight into a neighbor's house and called nine-one-one." Thelma squeezed Mrs. McGregor's hand reassuringly.

"Poor Mrs. McG," Bess said sympathetically as she watched the two women. "First her house was ruined, and now this."

"Do you think Nikos Manolotos is behind this?" George asked Nancy.

"I don't know," Nancy said. "But we'd better find out soon. Whoever is doing this is certainly serious about causing trouble for Mrs. McGregor."

Nancy watched as Thelma put an arm around Mrs. McGregor's shoulder. She saw the woman stiffen.

"Now don't you go feeling sorry for me, Thelma," Mrs. McGregor said, lifting her neighbor's arm away. "I'm just fine, and I'm sure the police will find whoever did this. There's nothing to worry about."

Bess leaned close to Nancy and whispered, "If this was supposed to scare Mrs. McG, it's not working. She's a real fighter."

As Bess spoke a blue police car pulled up to the curb with its lights flashing. An officer got out and started toward the foam-covered car. Nancy recognized Sergeant Benson, the same policewoman they had talked to that morning.

"Maybe the police will come up with something," Nancy said to George. George nodded and moved over to talk to Sergeant Benson.

Bess took a suspicious look around. "I'll stay close to Mrs. McG," she volunteered. "If someone wanted to hurt her, it would be easy to hide in this crowd."

Nancy and Bess walked over to their elderly friend. "Nancy, would you please tell Thelma that there's nothing to worry about?" Mrs. McGregor called to her.

Nancy forced a smile. "We'll get to the bottom of this," she said, trying to sound reassuring. Then, turning to Thelma, she asked, "Did you see any people near the car before the smoke?"

"No one," Thelma answered, shaking her head. "I had just turned the corner at the end of the block, and there was the car with all that black smoke billowing out."

"Maybe someone else saw something," Nancy said.

Mrs. McGregor looked over the crowd on the opposite sidewalk. She pointed to a blond woman with a baby in her arms and a two-year-old boy clinging to her leg.

"They live straight across the street," Mrs. McGregor said. "Suzie—that's the woman— spends quite a bit of time outside with her kids. Maybe she saw something."

Nancy hurried across the street and smiled as

she approached the young mother. "Excuse me, but did you see someone in the street before the smoke started?" Nancy asked. "I would really like to find out who did this to Mrs. McGregor."

The woman smiled weakly and shook her head. "Probably kids. Anyway, I'm afraid I'm no help."

Nancy thanked the woman and started away.

"Truck!" the little boy said loudly.

Nancy turned around to see the two-year-old pointing to an empty part of the street.

"Truck," he said again.

His mother laughed. "He really likes trucks," she said.

Nancy hesitated. Something told her there was an important clue in the boy's one word.

"Was there a truck there this morning?" she asked.

The woman thought for a moment.

"Truck!" the boy cried out again.

"Okay, okay," the woman said, patting her son's hand tenderly. Then, turning back to Nancy, she said, "I do remember a van there a few minutes ago—a plumber's van, I think."

"Do you remember what company it was from?" Nancy asked.

The woman frowned. "It was just a gray van with the word 'Plumbing' on it," she said.

Nancy's mind raced. There must be a connection between the damage at Mrs. McGregor's house and the smoke bomb in her car, she thought.

Bending down, Nancy gave the two-year-old a firm handshake. "Thanks—you're a good detective," she said.

The boy smiled back at Nancy and then buried his face shyly in his mother's pant leg.

Nancy hurried across the street. She was anxious to tell George and Bess what she had learned. The rest of the crowd had melted away, and the police car was pulling away from the curb.

Thelma was saying goodbye to Mrs. McGregor as Nancy crossed the lawn.

"If there's anything more I can do, just call me," Thelma said. "And I hope you get your plumbing fixed, too." She gave her neighbor's hand a final squeeze and started down the street.

Mrs. McGregor's face was a picture of surprise and confusion as Thelma walked away. After a moment she turned to Nancy. "Is there something wrong with my plumbing, too?" she asked.

"Thelma saw a plumbing van at your house this morning," Nancy explained.

"But I didn't call any plumbers," Mrs. McGregor said, shaking her head.

"Then it must have been the vandals," Bess said. She quickly explained their suspicions about the gray plumbing van.

"Let's all go inside to talk," Mrs. McGregor said with a sigh, motioning toward Mr. Bell's house. "I think I need to sit down before I hear any more." Nancy and Bess followed her toward the front door, where Mr. Bell and George met them.

Mr. Bell put a still-shaking arm around Mrs. McGregor's shoulder and guided her through the door. This time Mrs. McGregor didn't push the arm away. The girls followed them inside.

"I'll fix us something to drink while we talk," Mary McGregor said. While the girls seated themselves on a couch in the living room Mr. Bell followed Mrs. McGregor into the kitchen.

A moment later Nancy heard Mr. Bell's quiet but angry voice. "I told you not to talk to that newspaper reporter! All that stuff about pressuring the police to look for Nikos Manolotos—why do you keep stirring things up?"

"Horace, I can take care of myself," Mrs. McGregor replied firmly.

Nancy glanced at George and Bess. They, too, were listening. Bess raised her eyebrows, but before she could say anything the two older people reappeared. Mrs. McGregor was carrying glasses full of lemonade on a wooden tray.

Mrs. McGregor's smile seemed strained as she handed each girl a glass. Mr. Bell sat in his wooden rocking chair and dabbed his forehead

29

with the white handkerchief. He took the glass Mrs. McGregor handed him, but he didn't look her in the eye.

"Did you find a witness?" Bess asked Nancy, trying to sound enthusiastic.

"Not really," Nancy said, "but a woman and little boy across the street saw a van shortly before the smoke appeared."

"I bet the van was gray," George said.

"With 'Plumbing' on the side," Bess added.

"That's right," Nancy said. "So there is a connection between Mrs. McGregor's house being ransacked and the smoke bomb."

Nancy looked at Mrs. McGregor. For the first time that day the woman looked clearly shaken.

"I won't stop," Mrs. McGregor said, as though trying to convince herself. "I'm just not going to be scared. The recreation center is too important."

"Maybe you can help us find whoever is trying to scare you," Nancy said. "Do either of you remember seeing the van?"

Mr. Bell and Mrs. McGregor both shook their heads.

Watching Mr. Bell, Nancy noticed that he looked beaten and tired. His free hand reached down to pat Flip's head as the dog took up his post at Mr. Bell's side. Nancy noticed that the man's hand was shaking.

"Mr. Bell, are you sure you have no idea who's behind this?" Nancy pressed, looking the man directly in the eye.

Mr. Bell quickly shifted his gaze as he shook his head and said, "I don't know who it could be."

Did Mr. Bell know more than he was letting on? Nancy wondered. Or did he have something to hide?

"Sergeant Benson told me she found the remains of a smoke bomb under the hood of the car," George reported. "It looked like a small juice can blackened by soot. She said they work kind of like hand grenades. Someone probably just pulled the pin and dropped it under the hood. Once the can was opened, the smoke poured out."

"It sounds like a military item," Nancy reasoned.

"That's what Sergeant Benson said," George continued. "Smoke bombs can be purchased on the black market, mostly by professionals. But with a little money and the right connections, anyone can get them."

Nancy was sipping her lemonade, considering George's report, when Mr. Bell pushed himself to his feet. He shook his fist toward the window. "Now, look!" he shouted. "It's that darn Barnes boy."

31

Nancy turned and looked out the window. Two teenage boys were standing next to Mrs. McGregor's car. Each had a skateboard under one foot, and they seemed to be doing something to the hood of the car. One of them looked like the skateboarder Nancy had seen earlier, but she couldn't be sure.

Mr. Bell crossed the room stiffly and opened the front door. The taller boy looked up and pointed toward Mr. Bell. The shorter, red-haired boy jerked around in alarm. Then both jumped on their skateboards and careened down the street with a whirr of wheels.

"They sure took off in a hurry," Bess said, looking out the window.

"Too much of a hurry," Nancy said, frowning. She went quickly down the walk to check the car.

In the white film left by the fire-extinguisher foam someone had traced a message with a finger on the hood of the car. Nancy's heart jumped as she read the large block letters: "GOTCHA!"

4

A Mysterious Intruder

Nancy looked behind her to see the redheaded teenager and his friend speeding down the street on their skateboards. With expert balance the two jumped a curb onto the sidewalk and careened around the corner and out of sight.

George ran across the grass to join Nancy.

"It looks as if we have another suspect," Nancy said, pointing to the hood of the car. "I saw the shorter boy ride by when we first noticed the smoke bomb."

George looked at the letters. "But how are these boys connected to the van? They don't look old enough to drive."

"I don't know. Maybe Mr. Bell can tell us more," Nancy said, starting back toward the house. "He seemed to know one of the boys."

Mr. Bell was standing in the open doorway holding Flip in his arms when George and Nancy got back to the house.

"What were those boys doing?" Mr. Bell asked angrily as he held the door open for the girls.

"Now, Horace, I'm sure they were just looking at the car," Mrs. McGregor said.

Nancy and George exchanged worried looks.

"Actually, someone printed 'GOTCHA' on the hood of the car," George said slowly.

"I told you he was going to be trouble," Mr. Bell said. "He's no good."

"Which boy are you talking about?" Nancy asked Mr. Bell as she and George sat back down on the couch.

"The redhead," he said, waving his hand angrily toward the street. "Cory Barnes."

"I think I saw him ride by on his skateboard when we first noticed the smoke," Nancy said.

Mrs. McGregor stood up, shaking her head. "We don't need to drag Cory into this," she said. "Despite what you think, he's a good kid."

Mr. Bell took a deep breath and let it out in a long sigh. "All right, Mary, if that's the way you want it," he said, frowning. He got up and walked over to Mrs. McGregor, taking her hand gently.

Nancy could see that despite everything that

34

had happened, Mr. Bell and Mrs. McGregor shared a special closeness.

"How do you know Cory Barnes?" Nancy asked.

"He caused problems at the rec center all last winter," Mr. Bell said, his voice tinged with annoyance. "He's nothing but trouble."

Mrs. McGregor tugged impatiently on Mr. Bell's hand. "He's not a bad kid—he just likes excitement," she protested. "When I banned him from the rec center it was only to teach him some responsibility."

Bess's eyes got big. "You banned him from the rec center?" she asked.

"Yes. Last July he set off some firecrackers in a storage closet," Mrs. McGregor explained, sitting down again. "He scared some kids half to death. Even worse, it could have started a fire. I told him not to come back for three months."

"That could be a motive for smoke-bombing your car," Bess said, leaning forward with her elbows on her knees.

"I don't think so," Mrs. McGregor said. "He was very angry at me, but I can't believe he would do anything to hurt me. He never did come back to the rec center, so I got the impression he just wanted to avoid me."

"That would explain why he ran away from us just now," George said.

"Maybe. But that 'GOTCHA' could mean he set the smoke bomb and wanted to brag about it," Nancy pointed out.

"Cory Barnes." Bess formed the words carefully, as though trying to grasp their full meaning. "Could he be related to Cami Barnes, the leader of the Car Wash Kids?"

"Cami is his sister," Mrs. McGregor said, rocking gently in her chair. "And a nice girl, too."

Nancy guessed that Mrs. McGregor saw the good in everyone, but in the case of Cami, Nancy agreed wholeheartedly. She had met the eleven-year-old only once, but the girl was friendly and full of energy. She was also eager to help save the rec center. Cami had recruited a whole group of her friends to work at the fund-raising car wash.

"Cami should be at the car wash planning meeting tomorrow," Nancy said to Bess. "Maybe she will know something."

"I really don't think you need to waste your time on investigations," Mrs. McGregor said firmly, shaking her finger at Nancy. "You just concentrate on the fund-raising."

"I'll only ask a few questions." Nancy smiled and got to her feet. "Don't worry—it won't interfere with my work for the rec center."

Thanking Mr. Bell and Mrs. McGregor for the lemonade, the girls said goodbye and left the house.

"I feel sorry for Mrs. McG, having to go back to her ransacked house," Bess said as they climbed into Nancy's car. "Maybe we should help."

"I'm sure Mr. Bell will help her," Nancy said. "Besides, we can be of more help to Mrs. McGregor by tracking down whoever did those things."

After she dropped George and Bess off at their houses Nancy headed for home. It had been a day full of incidents—first the threatening note, then the ransacked house, then the smoke bomb, then the message drawn on the car. Nancy hoped to run the day's events past her father, Carson Drew, a well-known River Heights attorney. He and Nancy often helped each other on difficult cases.

But Nancy found the house empty. A note in the kitchen explained that her father was having dinner with a client. Hannah Gruen, the Drews' longtime housekeeper, had gone for a Sunday-evening visit with some friends.

Nancy was left to contemplate the day's mysteries by herself over a quick meal of leftover lasagna.

On Monday morning Nancy and George were hard at work again at the recycling center. It was almost three-thirty when Nancy arrived at the rec center for the car wash planning meeting.

After parking across the street, Nancy got out of her car. She paused to take a long look at the fire-blackened building. Big padlocks hung on the gymnasium doors, and the gym's large glass windows, broken in the fire, had been replaced by plywood.

Then Nancy saw Cami and Cory Barnes walking down the sidewalk toward a side entrance to the rec center. The door led to the part of the building that had survived the fire. A few rooms there were being used as headquarters for the fund-raising drive.

Cory wore a black T-shirt and jeans and carried his neon-green skateboard under his arm. His dark clothes contrasted with his sister's bright blue shirt and pants. But both kids had the same flame-colored hair.

Nancy was just crossing the street when she saw Cory hand something to Cami. Cami jumped backward. A large rubber spider fell to the sidewalk.

"Gotcha!" Cory said, laughing.

That was the same word that had been printed on Mrs. McGregor's car, Nancy realized.

Cami picked up the spider and tossed it back at Cory. "That wasn't funny, Cory," she said, her green eyes flashing. She glared as he rode his skateboard down the street.

Nancy called out Cami's name and waved to

her. Turning, Cami smiled and waited for Nancy. They walked together into the rec center.

The side entrance led into a narrow hallway with offices and meeting rooms on both sides. To the right of the door a small foyer had been turned into a makeshift reception area. The secretary, Sammie Sanders, sat there at her big wooden desk. Sammie was a middle-aged, motherly woman with light brown hair and a friendly smile.

Bess met Nancy and Cami in the hall and motioned for them to follow her.

"Sammie said we could use this room," Bess said brightly. As usual, Bess was full of energy.

"We're all ready," Cami reported as the girls pulled folding chairs around a small table. "I've got lots of kids signed up to work every afternoon this week and all day on Saturday. I wrote out who's working when on this schedule." She handed Nancy a sheet of notebook paper.

"What about the signs to publicize the car wash?" Bess asked.

"A bunch of us made signs over the weekend," Cami said. "We made enough to put them up at the corners at both ends of the block. Last week you gave me twenty-five dollars for supplies from the treasury, Bess. We only spent twenty-one dollars and forty-five cents—here's your change."

Nancy and Bess exchanged a smile as Cami carefully counted out the money on the table. "I think this car wash is going to be a winner," Nancy said warmly.

Cami smiled proudly.

When the girls had finished with their business Bess headed down the hall toward the reception desk. Nancy stayed behind to talk to Cami. "I saw Cory pull that prank on you earlier," Nancy said lightly. She didn't want to make Cami defensive. "I guess brothers can be annoying."

"Mine sure can be," Cami said. "And last summer things got worse. I think he was bummed out about missing karate."

"He knows karate?" Nancy said. She wondered how dangerous Cory could be as a fighter. Nancy herself was accomplished in karate, which she used only for defense. She knew, though, that some people used karate skills to bully others.

"Cory took lessons here at the rec center every summer except this last one," Cami said. "He's pretty good, really. He has a blue belt—that's two steps away from black." Nancy noticed that Cami sounded fond of her brother despite his teasing.

"Mrs. McGregor told me she banned him from the rec center," Nancy said, following Cami into the hall.

"Yes. He was pretty mad about that," Cami

said. "I know it wasn't Mrs. McG's fault, but Cory doesn't see it that way. He thinks she ruined his life."

"Has your brother been in any other trouble?" Nancy asked.

"Sometimes he has to stay after school, but that's about all," Cami told her. "Sometimes he can really try your patience, but he's not bad. He never hurts anyone. He's just a boy, you know?"

Nancy smiled and nodded her agreement. She wondered if both Mrs. McGregor and Cami could be wrong about Cory Barnes. Could he be dangerous?

"Hey, Nancy, how about helping me paint the thermometer?" Bess said, coming back down the hall with a can of paint and a paintbrush in her hand. "George called from the recycling center —we made another four hundred dollars today. And Mrs. McG got some donations in the mail, too."

"That's great news! But I'll let you handle the thermometer," Nancy said with a laugh. She knew that Bess hated climbing the twelve-foot ladder to paint the giant sign. "I really do need to check on something."

Bess shook her head and sighed in exaggerated disappointment. She walked with Cami out the front door.

Nancy went straight to the reception desk. "Sammie, where do you keep personnel records for the center?" she asked.

Sammie pointed toward two file cabinets shoved into a corner of the makeshift office. "That's all the records we saved from the fire, and they're pretty mixed up," she explained. "Good luck!"

It took Nancy several minutes of leafing through file folders to find the one labeled Nikos Manolotos.

When she opened it there was only one sheet of paper. On it was Nikos's name, address, and phone number.

"Is this all the information you keep on employees?" Nancy asked the secretary, showing her the folder.

"Why, no," Sammie said, looking surprised. "There should be a résumé with a work history and a list of references. But then, a lot was lost in the fire, and in the chaos that followed. Maybe the other pages fell out."

Nancy used the phone to call the number on the sheet. As she expected, the number had been disconnected. She jotted down the address and replaced the folder in the file cabinet.

Then Nancy walked outside and around to the front of the building. Bess was just climbing down from the ladder. The red line on the thermometer now reached to the twelve-hundred-dollar mark.

"We're still a long way from ten thousand dollars," Bess sighed, discouraged.

"It's a start," Nancy said to cheer her up. "We can celebrate over dinner."

The girls put away the ladder and paint, drove over to the recycling center, and picked up George. Then the three friends headed down the street in Nancy's car.

"This isn't the way to the Burger Barn," Bess said as Nancy turned down a narrow street in a run-down part of town.

"I want to drive by Nikos's house," Nancy explained. "It will only take a minute."

Nancy parked the car in front of a small brown house with peeling paint and a neglected yard. Newspapers had piled up on the front porch.

"I'll just be a minute," Nancy promised as she jumped out of the car. She went around the corner of the house, where she had to push her way through some overgrown shrubs. As she passed a window she saw a flash of light.

Carefully Nancy edged closer to the window and peered in. She saw the shadowy image of a person holding a small flashlight and sifting through papers at a desk.

The figure was too small to be Nikos Manolotos, and Nancy could see the silhouette of long hair.

It must be a woman, she thought—perhaps a friend of Nikos. Maybe that person could lead her to the fugitive!

Nancy noticed that an alley ran behind the house. She decided to check whether the person's car was parked there. But as she started to move a branch snagged her T-shirt.

Before she could stop it the branch snapped back against the wall of the house with a loud twang.

Nancy saw the dark shadow inside the house turn and hesitate. Then the intruder dashed toward the back of the house.

Nancy clawed past the overgrown shrubbery and fought her way clear. She was just in time to see the intruder slip out the back door and race across the yard toward a white convertible parked in the alley.

Nancy sprinted after her and managed to get a hand on the long, dark hair. The woman shrieked as Nancy grabbed at her hair and then reached around her shoulders. The two tumbled to the ground and rolled across the grass.

After a short struggle Nancy pinned the woman down with her knee. As the woman turned her face into the light of the street lamp, Nancy gasped.

She had tackled Ms. Stephanie Mann, chairwoman of the River Street rec center board of directors!

5

More Questions Raised

"Ms. Mann!" Nancy exclaimed, quickly backing off from the woman. She reached out her hand to help Stephanie up from the cold ground. In the dim light of the street lamp Nancy could see recognition in Stephanie's eyes. Even though Nancy had been to only a couple of board meetings, the chairwoman clearly knew who she was.

"Don't touch me, Nancy Drew!" Stephanie yelled, scrambling to her feet. "What do you think you're doing, attacking me that way?"

"I'm sorry," Nancy said. "I thought you were—" Nancy suddenly stopped, not knowing for sure how to finish. She still thought Stephanie was an intruder. Why else would she have run?

"I thought you might be a friend of Nikos Manolotos," Nancy said at last.

Nancy thought she saw a flash of panic in Stephanie's blazing black eyes, but it was quickly gone. The dark-haired woman lashed out again.

"What would that matter to you?" Stephanie demanded.

"I think he's been threatening a friend of mine," Nancy said. "I'd like to know where he is."

"I'd like to know where he is, too," Stephanie said. "But since I don't, I'm looking for evidence of the insurance payments. I don't know why I'm telling *you* this, though—I should be calling the police!"

Nancy stiffened. She didn't want to tell Stephanie she was investigating for Mrs. McGregor. Her eyes caught sight of some garbage cans and a box of old newspapers further down the alley. "I was just driving by checking for recyclables," Nancy lied. "When I saw you inside I got curious."

Stephanie looked Nancy over slowly and then suddenly became friendly. She smiled brightly as she brushed herself off. "I'm sorry if I snapped," she said, reaching out her hand. "I guess we're on the same team."

Nancy shook Stephanie's hand. It was nice to see a smile, but Nancy wondered if this was genuine friendliness or just good acting.

"You said you were looking for evidence of the insurance payments for the rec center," Nancy said. "But the insurance was never paid. How could you hope to find evidence of something that never happened?"

There was an awkward pause, and then Stephanie sighed. "Seeing that the insurance was paid was my responsibility as the chairwoman of the board. Mr. Manolotos assured me that everything was being done correctly. He even showed me canceled checks written to the insurance company." Stephanie paused to brush some grass from the sleeves of her dark sweater.

"Obviously the checks were fakes," she continued. "But I thought if I could find them, at least I could prove that I was doing my job. So I found an open window and went inside."

"Has anyone accused you of being responsible for the disappearing checks?" Nancy asked.

"No, but it could come up," Stephanie replied. "I have to protect my reputation."

Just then George and Bess came crashing through the shrubbery at the corner of the house. "We heard yelling," George said. "Is something wrong?"

"You're Stephanie Mann," Bess announced before anyone could answer. "I recognize you from your picture in the paper."

Stephanie showed a forced smile. Nancy guessed she would like to keep her adventure at Nikos's house a secret.

"Pleased to meet you, I'm sure," Stephanie said stiffly. She shook hands with Bess and George. Then Stephanie spoke in a low voice, looking each of the girls in the eyes. "Promise me none of you will tell anyone I was here tonight," she said. "It could ruin me!"

Bess and George promised. Nancy gave Stephanie an agreeable smile but said nothing.

Turning to Nancy, Stephanie said, "While I was in the house I looked for clues about where Nikos could have gone. I didn't find any, but I'll be sure and let you know if I hear anything new. You do the same for me, okay?"

"Of course," Nancy said, returning Stephanie's smile.

"Will I see you at the board meeting tomorrow?" Stephanie asked as she started toward her car.

"I'll be there," Nancy said. The three friends walked to the front of the house and watched as Stephanie drove down the narrow alley.

"Wow," Bess said after Stephanie was gone. "Imagine meeting Stephanie Mann at Nikos's house. I guess everybody's looking for him."

Nancy nodded and walked around the side of the house, opposite where she had been the first time. There was only one window.

"This must be where Stephanie got in," she said, pushing at the frame. It slid open freely.

"I guess her story checks out," Nancy said. She closed the window again and led the way to her car.

It was late when Nancy dropped her friends off after dinner and headed toward her own home. She arrived just as her father was going up to bed.

"On a case?" he asked when she came in. Carson had a way of knowing when Nancy was working on a mystery.

"Yes," Nancy said, giving her father a quick kiss on the cheek. "It seems to be the mystery of the disappearing suspect."

"Need an ear?" her father offered, tucking his newspaper under his arm. "I'd be glad to listen if it would help."

Nancy did want to talk to her father, but she could see that he was tired.

"It can wait," she said. "Except for one thing. Do you know Stephanie Mann?"

"The chairwoman of the River Street rec center board of directors?" Carson rubbed his chin thoughtfully. "She seems to be a very ambitious politician," he said. "I've heard that she plans to run for city council this year, and she wants to be mayor someday. Don't tell me *she's* a suspect!"

"Maybe," Nancy said. "Can we talk more tomorrow?"

"Sorry—I'm going out of town for a couple

days on business," Carson said with a frown. "How about lunch on Thursday? I'll ask Hannah to fix something special."

"It's a date," Nancy agreed. "I'll invite Bess and George."

It was almost one o'clock the next day when Nancy headed for the rec center to attend the board of directors meeting. She had spent the morning crushing aluminum cans at the recycling center, and then she and George had eaten a quick lunch at the Burger Barn.

When she got to the rec center Cami Barnes was coming out the door. Under her arm was a stack of cardboard posters.

"Look, Nancy—the signs for the car wash," Cami said. "Aren't they great?"

Nancy grinned and nodded. "Those should really bring in customers," she said.

Cami skipped across the street to the vacant lot where the car wash would be. Nancy went inside the rec center. Sammie Sanders smiled at Nancy and pointed down the hall to the meeting room where the directors were gathering.

Four of the board members were already there, sitting at the long table in the front of the room. A dozen other people, including Bess, George, and Mrs. McGregor, sat in folding chairs arranged in two rows in front of the table. Nancy joined them.

Then Stephanie Mann hurried into the room and sat in the center seat at the long table.

"Let's get started," Stephanie Mann said brightly, tapping her gavel on the table. She smiled warmly in Nancy's direction. "Why don't we begin with you, Ms. Drew. Do you have a report?"

Nancy stood and gave a brief rundown of the youth fund-raising efforts. Using notes that Bess had prepared, she reported that earnings from the recycling so far had brought the total to sixteen hundred dollars. "The car wash starts this afternoon, and we have the karaoke contest tomorrow," she added. "Those events will bring the total up even higher."

Next Mary McGregor stood and reported on the senior citizens' efforts. "We have a lot of people working on crafts and baked goods to sell at the bazaar starting tomorrow," she said. "We think that will be a good money-maker. And we've already sold two thirds of the tickets to the dinner on Saturday."

"That's nice," Stephanie said when they had finished. "But we're still a long way from our goal."

She paused and then continued. "I've got some big news that should change everything. The reason I was a little late today was that I've just received an offer that will save the rec center. Mr.

51

Jerry Hartley, one of our local businessmen, has offered to buy the rec center for one hundred thousand dollars."

The other board members looked surprised. Stephanie hurried on.

"With that money we could buy a new lot outside of town, where the land is less expensive. And there would still be money left over for the building fund. I hope the board will accept this offer."

For a long moment the room was quiet. Nancy could see several townspeople shaking their heads. At the conference table the board members conferred quietly. Stephanie glanced around the room, a worried look on her face.

Mrs. McGregor rose to her feet. She wore a determined expression. "You can't move the rec center," she said. "The reason it's been a success is that it's in the center of town, where kids and seniors can reach it easily without needing to drive. It's been here for more than eighty years!"

Just then Nancy smelled smoke. She looked around and saw a few black wisps trailing out of an air vent near the back of the room. Bess grabbed her friend's arm and said, "I smell smoke, Nancy."

In another moment a thick black cloud began to roll out of the vent. "Fire!" someone yelled, and everyone stampeded toward the door.

6

The Deadline Is Set

Nancy, Bess, and George hurried for the door, trying to remain calm in the panic to leave the building.

"I knew this place wasn't safe," an angry voice said. Nancy recognized it as Stephanie Mann's, though she could not see the woman in the crowd rushing for the exit.

Luckily, the hallway seemed less smoky than the meeting room. Nancy led the way outdoors. The secretary and the few other people who had been in the rec center were already outside on the sidewalk. Within minutes a fire truck pulled up to the curb.

The fire fighters charged into the building. One man was stationed near the door to prevent anyone from entering.

Soon one fire fighter came back out. "There's no sign of flames," Nancy heard him tell the fireman guarding the door. "But don't let anyone back in until we've discovered what caused the smoke."

"Come with me," Nancy said quietly, motioning to Bess and George. "I've got an idea about what caused this."

The girls slipped away from the crowd and around the brick building. Nancy opened the back door carefully. She ducked inside and opened the first door on the left side of the hall.

"The chief told us not to come in here," Bess whispered, tugging on Nancy's sleeve. "This could be dangerous."

"Not if the smoke was what I think it was," Nancy said, stepping into the small, dusty furnace room. She scanned the network of heat ducts and electrical wires. "The firemen are looking in the smoky rooms. But I think the source of the trouble may be here."

Nancy pointed to the aluminum pipe that carried warm air to the other rooms of the building. There was a small sliding door in the side of the pipe. Nancy opened it and found a dark canister inside.

"A smoke bomb, just like the one used on Mrs. McGregor's car!" George exclaimed.

Nancy nodded. "The smoke was carried

through the pipes into the meeting room. Someone must have put this here to disrupt the meeting."

"Does this mean Nikos was here?" George asked.

"He is our best suspect," Nancy said. "But anyone could have come in the back door and left the smoke bomb—including Cory Barnes."

George and Bess went to report their discovery to the fire fighters. One team of fire fighters examined the furnace room, while others set up a large fan in the doorway to help clear the smoke. George and Bess joined the relieved group of people milling around on the sidewalk outside.

Meanwhile, Nancy slipped around the back of the rec center. Behind the building the city had turned a narrow band of shrubs and trees into a nature trail. Despite the commotion at the front of the building, it was still quite peaceful in back.

Nancy could see nothing suspicious. She was about to go inside when she spotted Horace Bell walking along the nature trail with Flip.

"Hello, Mr. Bell," Nancy said, walking toward the path.

"Oh—hello, Nancy." Mr. Bell looked startled. "Is the meeting over?"

Nancy realized that Mr. Bell followed Mrs. McGregor's activities very closely.

"No," Nancy said slowly. "But I'm afraid there

was a minor problem. Someone put a smoke bomb in the air vent. We all had to leave the building for a while."

Mr. Bell looked suddenly shaken. His face went white, and he clenched his fist around the dog leash.

"Everything's okay now," Nancy said. "But I wondered if you had seen anyone while you were walking."

"No one," he said. "Flip and I left Mary here about half an hour ago. Then we walked to the end of the trail, and we've just come back."

"Do you walk here often?" Nancy asked.

"Morning and night," Mr. Bell said, looking down at his dog. "Flip and I need our exercise. Is Mary okay?"

"Everyone's fine," Nancy reassured him. "Mrs. McGregor's probably still waiting with the others on the sidewalk in front, if you want to see her."

Mr. Bell hesitated. "I'll talk to her later," he said at last. He reached down to pat Flip and started back down the path.

Nancy went around to the front. A fire fighter was carrying the smoke bomb toward the truck. Nancy told him that Horace Bell had not seen anyone come or go along the nature trail.

"I'm not surprised," said the fire fighter. "There would have been a slight delay between the time this thing went off and the time the smoke got to the meeting room. Whoever did it is probably long gone."

The fire fighters climbed back into their truck and drove away. Meanwhile, the danger over, the board members and volunteers were gathered on the sidewalk continuing their heated discussion. Nancy stood on the edge of the little crowd, listening.

Stephanie Mann clearly had not been swayed by Mrs. McGregor's objections. "This old building is pretty nearly worthless," she insisted. "Mr. Hartley's offer is quite generous. We mustn't pass up this opportunity."

Stephanie glanced at her fellow board members. Nancy guessed she was trying to determine which ones would support her idea. Nancy saw a faint smile on Stephanie's face as three of the other four board members nodded their agreement.

Mrs. McGregor's face was flushed with anger. "If we move the rec center out of town, it won't be used by the people who need it most—young people and seniors who don't have cars."

"That's right," Bess said, pushing her way forward. "And the fund-raising drive is going well. We just need more time."

"According to your own figures, Miss Marvin," Stephanie began firmly, "you're still far from reaching the goal for our start-up fund."

"But once the plans are approved there will be grants available to provide the rest of the money for the building," Bess said anxiously.

Stephanie Mann shrugged. "Mr. Hartley has given us eight days to make our decision or the offer will be withdrawn," she said. "Unless you can meet the fund-raising goal before our meeting next week, I think the board will have to accept his offer." And with a curt nod she turned her back and stalked away.

Still muttering among themselves, the board members and volunteers wandered off in several directions.

Nancy, George, and Bess followed Mrs. McGregor to her temporary office, a small cubicle just across from the furnace room. It had been a storage room before the fire. Mrs. McGregor had managed to cram the few things salvaged from her burned office into the smaller space.

A metal desk filled most of the room. There was one additional chair pushed against the wall by the door, and boxes were stacked in the corners.

Mrs. McGregor sat down in the chair behind her desk. Bess pulled up the other chair, and Nancy and George leaned against the wall.

"I'm afraid we won't be able to raise eight thousand four hundred dollars by next week," Mrs. McGregor said, sighing.

"We have to try, at least," Bess said.

Mrs. McGregor smiled. "Yes, I know," she said. "I just wish I felt more confident that we will succeed."

Then, leaning forward in her chair, she looked down at her desk. "What's this?" she asked. She picked up a plain white envelope with her name written on the front.

Opening the envelope, Mrs. McGregor read the note inside. She dropped it to her desk as though it had burned her fingers.

On a piece of plain yellow note paper, printed in pencil, was a message: WHERE THERE'S SMOKE, THERE'S FIRE. DON'T BE THE NEXT TO GET BURNED.

Nancy examined the note carefully.

"It looks the same as the one I found in the magazine," Bess said, looking over Nancy's shoulder.

"Yes, I'd say both the paper and the printing are a match," Nancy said. "See how it's written in all capital letters."

"And the lines are all very straight," George observed. "Do you think it was Nikos?"

Nancy thought a moment. If Nikos was in hiding, why would he risk coming to the rec center? she wondered.

"Mrs. McGregor, is there anyone else who might want to frighten you?" Nancy asked.

59

"I can't think who," Mrs. McGregor said, raising her hands in confusion. "I hope you're not going to accuse Cory Barnes."

"He *is* a suspect," Nancy said.

"Not on my list," Mrs. McGregor said firmly. "Anyway, I won't be frightened, and I won't give up." Mrs. McGregor straightened in her chair. She once again looked like the strong and determined woman Nancy knew.

"And I hope none of you girls will give up either," she said, looking at each of the girls in turn. "I'm going to need your help to meet our goal for next week."

"Of course we'll help," Nancy said. "But I think you should take these threats seriously." She could see that even though Mrs. McGregor was trying to brush off her fear, her face was pale.

"I'll be careful," Mrs. McGregor said, managing a small laugh. "Now let's get back to work." She began to sort through some papers on her desk, as if to tell the girls it was time for them to leave.

With Mrs. McGregor's permission Nancy put the threatening note in her pocket and followed George and Bess out the door.

"I guess we need to see how things are going at the car wash," Nancy said. She led the way down the hallway. As soon as she and her friends stepped out the door onto the street, Nancy knew they had a problem.

"Where are all the cars?" George asked, looking across the street to the vacant lot.

"Where are all the kids?" Bess added.

Nancy had hoped to see the lot full of cars waiting to be washed. Instead it was nearly deserted. Cami Barnes and two other girls sat at a small table waiting for business.

Nancy and her friends crossed the street.

"Where is everybody?" George asked.

"Have you made any money?" Nancy asked.

"We've only washed two cars," Cami said, discouraged. "And both of those belonged to the parents of kids who are working here."

"But I thought this would be a good money-maker," Bess said.

"So did we." Cami sighed. "Most of the kids got so bored they went across the street to shop."

She pointed to the large warehouse next to the rec center, which had been converted into a mini-mall of small shops.

Nancy looked up and down the street. "Maybe we should check on the signs," she said. "Bess and I can walk to the corner near the rec center. George can check the signs at the other end of the block."

Once Nancy got to the corner she quickly saw

the problem. There should have been a large sign next to the street on the rec center lot, and a smaller one across the street pointing in the direction of the car wash. Both were gone.

Then Nancy heard the crackle of flames. Turning around, she saw a small bonfire on the gravel lot near the street. Cory Barnes stood next to the fire, poking at it with a long stick.

"What could he be burning?" Bess asked.

"I don't know," Nancy said, starting toward the fire. "Let's find out."

Nancy took a dozen steps before she recognized one of the large squares of cardboard on the fire. It was white poster board on a wooden frame, painted with bright blue letters.

Cory Barnes was burning the car wash signs!

7

Danger Lurks

"What are you doing?" Bess yelled. She broke into a run across the lot toward the small fire.

Nancy hurried behind her, but Bess got to Cory Barnes first. "How could you steal our signs and burn them this way?" she demanded.

"I didn't! Someone else built the fire. I was just riding my skateboard down the street and saw it," a surprised Cory stammered. "I came to watch over it and make sure no sparks blew into the bushes."

"Just like the other day at Mary McGregor's house," Nancy said, working hard to control her anger. "You just happened to be riding by then, too, right after the smoke bomb went off."

"Wait a minute," Cory protested nervously. "I admit writing that word on Mrs. McG's car, but I never set any smoke bombs. I'm steamed at her, sure, but I wouldn't do anything like that."

"Oh, Cory, stop playing innocent," Bess said angrily. "And stop hassling Mrs. McG. She's working to save the rec center for all of us. After all, the center used to be a fun place for you, too."

"That was before Mrs. McGregor ruined it for me," Cory shot back.

Bess didn't back off. "Stop blaming her for your problems."

Cory gave Bess a blank look. Without another word he dropped the stick into the fire and picked up his skateboard. He shot one last cold look at Bess and walked to the sidewalk. A moment later he was on his skateboard, gliding away down the street.

"Sorry," Bess said sheepishly. "I suppose you wanted to ask him some questions."

"You did all right, Bess," Nancy said. "I did have a couple of things to ask him, though."

"Do you think Cory Barnes is behind all the problems?" Bess asked as they headed back toward the rec center.

"After what he wrote on Mrs. McG's car, and being here today, he certainly is a suspect," Nancy said. "He has a motive."

The two girls walked quickly to where George

and Cami were waiting on the sidewalk in front of the rec center.

"The signs are all gone," George said.

"We know. We saw Cory on the other side of the building," Nancy said, watching Cami as she spoke. "He was standing over a fire—it was the signs burning. But he said someone else started the fire."

Cami's face turned red. "My brother wouldn't take the signs," Cami insisted. "And he doesn't lie. If he said someone else started that fire, then it's true."

"I hope you're right," Nancy said. She really meant it. She knew it would hurt Cami to find out her brother was involved with the rec center problems.

Nancy suggested that Cami go into the mini-mall and round up the rest of the Car Wash Kids. Bess and George got some cardboard and poster paints from Sammie and quickly made some signs.

Twenty minutes later the first customer pulled into the car wash. Just in time Cami ran down the sidewalk with a dozen of her friends.

"We might make our goal yet," Bess said as she grabbed a bucket full of soapy water.

The Car Wash Kids went to work. One group washed the cars with soft sponges while another used hoses to rinse them off. Four others used chamois cloths to dry the cars to a bright shine.

The owners of the first two cars both gave an extra dollar to the fund and promised to tell their friends about the car wash.

"That's what we need to really get this thing going," Bess said, dropping her sponge in a bucket with a splash. "We need to *tell* people about the car wash."

Nancy and George smiled at Bess's enthusiasm.

"What do you want us to do, run through the streets yelling?" George asked.

"Better," Bess said. "Let's go to the radio station. I bet if we explained, the deejay at WQBM would put us on the air."

"Great idea," George said. "It's just around the corner."

"You two go ahead. I'll listen to you on the radio," Nancy said with a laugh. "I need to run some errands." She had promised Hannah she would stop by the supermarket and pick up some groceries.

Nancy was just pulling into her driveway with her groceries when she heard the disc jockey on WQBM with a special announcement.

"This is Crazy Conrad, bringing you important news about River Heights's own River Street Recreation Center," the voice on the radio said.

The deejay introduced Bess and George and asked each to talk.

"You can get your car cleaned and help save the rec center at the same time," Bess said.

"It's just five dollars, and the Car Wash Kids guarantee satisfaction," George chimed in.

Nancy smiled. Her friends sounded almost like professionals. She was sure business would pick up at the car wash after that.

When the announcement was over the deejay put on another hit record. Nancy turned off the car motor and carried her bags inside. After putting everything away she fixed a light supper and sat down with the nightly newspaper.

On the front page was a photo of Stephanie Mann. Nancy read the story with interest.

Stephanie had announced that she was running for the city council. No wonder she had wanted to protect her reputation when she was caught snooping at Manolotos's house, Nancy thought. A scandal could ruin her chances of winning the election.

Nancy picked George up at her house the next morning to take her to the recycling center. When they arrived a truck loaded with cardboard was waiting for the gates to open. Nancy parked and locked her car. Out of the corner of her eye she spotted a gray van pulling out of a side street across from the center.

Nancy whirled around, pointing at the van. "Look, George!" she called out. She could only see the back doors of the van as it drove away.

"I wish we could have seen the sides of that van," she said, frustrated. "These days I check every gray van I see for the word 'Plumbing.'"

"I know what you mean," George said. "Too bad we were already parked. We could have driven after it."

"Probably nothing to worry about," Nancy said, but as they walked toward the recycling center gates she felt uneasy.

Nancy and George passed through a narrow opening beside the main gate and went into the recycling center lot. Inside the stocky manager was directing volunteers as they prepared to open for the day.

"I need someone to operate the cardboard compactor," he said as the girls approached.

"I'll do it," Nancy said with a smile. She always liked doing new things.

The manager led the way up the steps to a small platform overlooking the huge compactor. The manager showed Nancy the on-and-off switch on the left side of the platform. He gave her a long metal pole to push loose any cardboard that got stuck on its way to the crusher.

After a quick lesson in safety Nancy pushed a button, and the huge compactor rumbled to life.

Another worker jumped on the forklift and began pushing cardboard onto the four-foot-wide conveyor belt. The cardboard crawled and lurched forward until it dropped into a huge square metal-sided pit.

One wall of the pit moved back and forth in slow, even piston actions as it crushed the cardboard. A metal railing in front of Nancy kept her from falling into the powerful jaws of the machine.

Nancy watched as cardboard tumbled into the crusher. A large box the size of a refrigerator jammed against the far corner of the conveyor belt. Other cardboard began to back up behind it.

Nancy leaned against the railing and jabbed forcefully at the box with the metal pole. As she did she felt the railing give way beneath her.

Nancy cried out as she tumbled into the crusher. She hit the bottom hard.

Nancy looked up in time to see the far wall begin to close in on her. "Help!" she screamed.

8

A Clue in the Ashes

Nancy scrambled to her feet inside the metal box of the compactor. Again she cried, "Help!" The roar of the machine was deafening. She wondered if anyone had heard her cry.

Nancy fought back a wave of panic as the wall moved toward her. There were only a few feet left before she would be crushed into the bale of cardboard!

She looked for something to grab to pull herself out, but with the railing gone there was nothing. She clawed at the metal sides of the box but could not get a handhold.

Nancy closed her eyes and yelled as loud as she could into the open air above her.

When her eyes snapped open she saw George

scrambling up the ladder to the platform. Reaching the top, George stood there stunned, not sure how to help Nancy.

"The switch!" Nancy yelled. Her words jarred George into action. Whirling on the platform, George searched for the button that would stop the treacherous machine.

"Where is it?" she cried, turning back to Nancy.

Nancy knew there was no more time. The wall was already crowding her and coming closer with each second. She clawed again at the wall of the compactor.

"Here!" George yelled, leaning over the side. Bracing herself with the remaining railing, George reached out her hand. Nancy gripped it hard and pulled herself up.

Nancy scrambled to the platform and rolled onto her stomach in time to see the cardboard crushed mercilessly just below her.

"That was close," George said.

"Too close," Nancy said shakily. She got to her feet and fumbled for the off button. The machine slowly ground to a halt.

"Are you all right?" George asked.

Nancy nodded and brushed herself off.

After she caught her breath Nancy looked at the metal posts that had held the railing. They

71

were broken off in an even line. Nancy noticed scrapes on the remaining metal—marks that could only have come from a saw.

"This was no accident," Nancy said. "Someone sawed through those posts, knowing they would break when anyone leaned on the railing."

Nancy and George climbed down from the platform. The forklift driver raced toward them, with the manager right behind him. After making sure that Nancy and George were both unhurt the manager climbed up the ladder to the crusher and examined the broken railing.

When he climbed back down the manager's face was serious. "That railing was cut," he said. "I'm closing the recycling center down while we check for any other sabotage."

"But you can't," George protested. "We need the money for the rec center."

"I don't have any choice," the agitated manager said. "We can't operate the cardboard compactor without the railing, and I can't risk anyone else getting hurt."

"I'm afraid he's right," Nancy said. "I know he'll get things started again as soon as it's safe."

George sighed.

Nancy started toward the gate of the recycling center. "I know what we can do while we wait. I've been wanting some time to talk to Jerry Hartley," she said to George.

"Do you think Jerry Hartley's been threatening Mrs. McGregor?" George asked as they walked to Nancy's car.

"I don't know. But if he wants the property badly enough, he might try to stop the fund-raising drive," Nancy reasoned.

Nancy had often driven past the large, five-story brick office building that had the name of Hartley Enterprises, Inc., painted in large green letters on its side. Now she headed there with George. They parked in front and climbed out of the car.

Scanning the directory in the lobby, Nancy saw that the executive offices were on the fifth floor.

The two girls stepped into the elevator. Nancy pushed the button for the top floor.

"We're here to see Mr. Hartley," Nancy told the slender secretary on the top floor.

"Do you have an appointment?" the secretary asked.

"I'm afraid not," Nancy said. "But tell him I'm here about the rec center."

"I'll see," the secretary said. She disappeared through an inner door.

A moment later she reappeared. "Mr. Hartley will see you now," she said.

Nancy and George followed her into a large, comfortable office with a white carpet and several modern paintings on the wall.

An average-height man in an expensive business suit sprang to his feet. Jerry Hartley smiled brightly as Nancy introduced herself. He reached out to shake hands first with Nancy and then with George. Nancy thought that he looked a little like a big, friendly bear—slightly overweight, with wavy brown hair.

"I'm curious why you want the River Street rec center," Nancy said as she and George sat down.

Mr. Hartley walked around his desk to a big leather chair. He leaned forward and rested his elbows on his desk.

"I already own the mini-mall on River Street, next to the rec center," Mr. Hartley said, still smiling. "It's becoming a busy place. I desperately need more parking."

"You're buying the rec center to make a parking lot?" George said in disbelief.

"That's right," Mr. Hartley said matter-of-factly. "I plan to tear down what's left of the building and pave the whole lot. I think it will increase the number of shoppers at the mall significantly."

"Couldn't you use the vacant lot across the street?" Nancy asked, thinking of the lot they were using for the car wash.

"That's certainly an option," Mr. Hartley said. "But the rec center lot is on the same side of the street as my mini-mall. It would be much more convenient for shoppers—they wouldn't have to cross the street. I'm sure you understand."

Nancy did understand. Mr. Hartley thought he was making a sound business decision, but it wasn't necessarily good for people.

"But the rec center is important to the community," Nancy argued.

"I hoped my offer would help the rec center as well as my mall," Hartley said, tapping his pen on his desk casually. "I thought the money would help you build a nice new recreation center out of town."

"But the rec center should stay in town where the people are," George said, a hint of anger in her voice.

Jerry Hartley leaned back in his chair and looked straight at the girls. His smile never wavered. "If you can raise enough money to keep the rec center in town, I don't want to interfere with that," he said. "If you can't, then my offer will be good for everybody."

Hartley rose from his chair abruptly, an action that signaled Nancy and George to leave.

"He certainly seemed friendly," George said when they were alone in the elevator. "It's hard to suspect him of any wrongdoing."

"Yes, and everything he said made sense," Nancy said. "But let's not count him out as a suspect yet. Looks can be deceiving."

After leaving the building Nancy dropped George off at the recycling center. To their disappointment, the manager still hadn't opened the gates for business.

Nancy drove on to the rec center. She wanted to check on the senior citizens' bazaar, which had started that afternoon.

When she walked in Nancy saw that the place was packed. Tables had been set up in three large rooms along the ground-floor hallway. Some of the tables were piled high with cookies, pies, cakes, and all sorts of other baked goods. Others had craft items, many with a holiday theme. Christmas stockings and tree ornaments seemed to be favorites. But there were also strings of colorful beads and tie-dyed T-shirts made by younger artists.

Bess was sitting with a metal money box at the cashier's table in the hallway. "Nancy, I'm so glad you came," Bess called out to her friend. "We're doing great business."

"I'm glad you're doing well," Nancy said. "I'm afraid there's been trouble at the recycling center." She told Bess about the accident.

"The sabotage couldn't have been aimed at Mrs. McGregor," Bess said. "She wasn't even there."

"I know," Nancy agreed. "But it did shut down

76

the recycling business. I think someone may be out to stop the fund-raising drive."

"But that doesn't explain why Mrs. McGregor was threatened," Bess pointed out. "Or why smoke bombs were put in her car and in the rec center heat vents."

"Maybe this mystery is deeper than it first appeared," Nancy mused. "I'm going to talk to Mrs. McGregor again. I feel like we're overlooking something."

Nancy found Mrs. McGregor in her temporary office by the furnace room. Nancy brought her up to date on the trouble at the recycling center and recounted her meeting with Jerry Hartley. Then she raised a sensitive question.

"Did you ever figure out who left the papers by the space heater that started the rec center fire?" Nancy asked.

Mrs. McGregor's concern showed on her face. "No. But it certainly wasn't me," she said, lacing her fingers together. "I know some people don't believe that. But I would never do anything that careless. And I certainly wouldn't lie about it."

"Can you think of anyone who would have started the fire on purpose?" Nancy asked. She was thinking of Cory Barnes and the firecrackers, and of Jerry Hartley wanting to buy the rec center land. She even had to wonder about

Stephanie Mann. The politician seemed too eager to sell the rec center.

"Certainly not," Mrs. McGregor said, bristling. "The fire here was an accident. I don't know how it happened, but no one here would intentionally burn the building."

Nancy knew she had nothing to gain by arguing with Mrs. McGregor. She thanked her for her time and left the small office.

Down the hall people were still working their way from room to room at the bazaar. Nancy turned in the opposite direction. She hoped no one would notice when she slipped under the yellow tape blocking a second hallway. Ignoring the words on the tape that read Fire Scene, Do Not Cross, she walked down the deserted hall into the burned portion of the building.

The hallway showed little damage from the fire, except for black streaks around each of the doors where smoke had seeped out. The smoke damage was heaviest around the door to Mrs. McGregor's old office at the end of the hall. Mrs. McGregor's name plate was still on the door, partly blackened.

Nancy opened the door carefully. The inside of Mrs. McGregor's office was completely charred. Nancy looked carefully at the brick wall that ran along the outside of the building. It was undamaged. Though the bricks were blackened, Nancy was confident they were still strong enough to support the building.

The office's other three walls, however, had been built of wood. Some were burned completely away. Through a gaping hole at the back of the office Nancy could see the old gymnasium.

She walked gingerly across the floor. The wood beneath her feet was the only part of the room that wasn't black. Nancy was reminded how quickly fire climbs skyward.

She stepped through the hole in the back wall of the room and stood in the charred gymnasium. The only light came through a row of windows along the top of the high wall. Black with soot, they let in filtered rays of sun.

On the ceiling, soot-covered light fixtures hung from bare electrical wires. The plastic covering on the wires had completely melted away in the fire.

The wooden floor was buckled from the water used to fight the fire. Ash and soot had mixed with the water and dried to a hard black crust.

It was difficult for Nancy to remember this room as it had been, filled with the laughter of teens playing volleyball or practicing karate.

Nancy stepped back through the opening and examined Mrs. McGregor's office. A blackened oak desk still stood in the middle of the room. Nancy could see that the drawers had been opened and the papers inside removed. To her right she saw the space heater that had apparently started the fire.

The ashes of a stack of papers lay in front of the heater. Despite the fire, the papers had held their shape, but now they were fragile sheets of black that would crumble if touched. Nancy could see that the flames had started there and climbed the walls to the ceiling.

As she scanned the charred room Nancy had little hope of finding any clues as to who might have started the fire, or why. But then, as she was about to leave, Nancy's trained eyes caught sight of something out of place. The space heater and burned papers were just as the newspaper had described—except for one thing.

The heater's cord lay coiled on the soot-covered floor. It was not plugged into the wall outlet.

An unplugged space heater could not have started the blaze, Nancy knew. Was it possible that the rec center fire was the result of arson?

9

Thief in the Dark

Nancy bent down close to the space heater. There were no marks in the soot to indicate that the cord had been moved since the fire.

Pondering this new evidence, Nancy stepped carefully out of the charred office. She walked down the deserted hall and ducked under the yellow tape, checking to be sure she wasn't seen.

She passed the crowd at the bazaar and pushed open the side door of the rec center.

Out front Bess was painting the new fund-raising total on the thermometer. The red line was up to $3,500. Not bad, Nancy thought, but still $6,500 short of the goal.

"I'm starved," Bess said, jumping down from her ladder. "How about dinner?"

"Good idea," Nancy said, smiling. "I could use some food and a rest before the karaoke starts."

The girls got in Nancy's car and drove to the recycling center to pick up George.

"I have good news," George said, climbing into the car. "The cardboard compactor is fixed. The recycling center will open as usual tomorrow morning. The manager is posting a guard there tonight to help keep things safe."

"That's good. We'll need the recycling money if we're going to make our goal," Bess said as they drove toward the Burger Barn.

After they had ordered their burgers and fries Nancy told her friends about the unplugged space heater in Mrs. McGregor's old office.

"Do you think the fire was caused by arson?" Bess asked.

"If someone really is trying to stop the fundraising, it could be someone who wants the rec center out of the way," Nancy reasoned.

"That would make Jerry Hartley a suspect," Bess said. "If he wanted the land for a parking lot, burning the rec center would be a first step."

"He definitely has a motive," George said. "There's also Nikos Manolotos."

"Yes," Nancy said. "But why would he want to stop the fund-raising drive? I'd think he would want the building rebuilt so people would forget about his crime."

"Nikos could be trying to scare Mrs. McG into leaving him alone," George suggested.

"Yes—though if that's his plan, it's not working," Nancy noted.

"What about Cory Barnes?" Bess asked. "He seems to show up every time something goes wrong."

"True," Nancy said. "He could want to get even with Mrs. McGregor for banning him from the rec center."

"The fire did start in Mrs. McG's office," Bess pointed out. "Maybe he wanted her to be blamed. That would give him revenge."

"But we also have the gray van with 'Plumbing' on the side, and Cory is too young to drive," Nancy added.

"Is there anyone else?" Bess asked.

Nancy took a bite of her hamburger and thought for a minute.

"Stephanie Mann," she said with a shrug.

"She certainly seems determined to sell the rec center," George said.

"That seems odd—moving the center out of town could cost her votes in the city council election," Nancy said. "But the other board members seem to agree with her. Maybe they really do think they are doing what is best."

"What about Horace Bell?" Bess asked. "I

don't think he likes Nancy's investigating very much."

"He's been hard to get along with, all right," Nancy agreed. "But he doesn't seem to have a motive. And he was sitting in his house with us when the first smoke bomb was planted in Mrs. McGregor's car."

Nancy gazed out the window as she let her mind go over the details. "All in all, it's a baffling case," she said, pushing her tray away. "I'm not very close to solving it, and meanwhile Mrs. McGregor and the rec center are both in danger."

As they cleared the cups and papers from the table Bess looked at her watch. "I'm late for the karaoke fund-raiser," she cried in alarm. "I'm supposed to collect the money from kids who want to sing with the karaoke machine. Thank goodness Cami will be there to cover for me."

Bess jumped to her feet as she spoke and quickly dumped the cups and papers from the table into a garbage can. She was the first one back to Nancy's car.

When they got back to the rec center the last of the bazaar customers were filtering out the doors, and the bazaar was closing for the night.

As soon as they walked in the door the girls could hear the friendly rhythm of rock music.

"I hope there's a crowd," Bess said. The three

84

girls headed upstairs to a large room on the top floor of the rec center.

Nancy could feel her mood start to brighten as she neared the source of the music. From the top of the stairs she saw the room lined with boys and girls tapping their feet and swaying to the music.

Cory Barnes stood with some other boys against one wall. He was pretending to play an electric guitar while his friends cheered him on.

Cami sat at a small table in the corner with a stack of numbered tickets in front of her. The metal money box sat on the table in front of her.

"Sorry I'm late!" Bess rushed up breathlessly. "Have you taken in many donations?"

"I'm afraid not," Cami said, discouraged. "There are lots of people here, and everybody seems to like the music. But no one is doing the karaoke."

Nancy looked around. The kids in the room were gathered in small groups. Some were talking among themselves, and others were just listening to the music.

Next to Cami's table a young man who introduced himself to the crowd as Ryan was operating the karaoke machine. He had volunteered his time and equipment for the fund-raiser.

Music rocked from large speakers, and the words to the songs appeared on a small television screen, but no one was singing. A bright pink microphone hung, unused, on its stand.

"It looks like fun," said Nancy.

"I'm sure it would be," Cami said. "I think everyone's afraid to be first."

"We've got to do something," George said, "or this is going to be a flop."

"Why don't we sing the first song?" Bess said. She reached into her pocket and pulled out a five-dollar bill. "Let me be the first to donate to the fund."

Bess pulled Nancy and George over to the karaoke machine.

"At last, some singers!" Ryan exclaimed. Nancy wasn't sure if it was enthusiasm or desperation that she heard in his voice.

"What song would you like?" Ryan yelled to be heard over the music. When Nancy, George, and Bess just looked at one another blankly, he shoved a thick magazine at them.

Flipping through the pages, Nancy saw that it was full of song titles.

"I can play any of these," Ryan said. "Pick a good one so we can really get this place rockin'."

The girls flipped through the pages, passing over songs recorded by various artists, from the Beatles to Bonnie Raitt.

"This is it!" Bess shrieked at last. Her finger stopped under "Star Struck and Ready to Rock," the hit single by a new group called the Lavender Dreamers.

"Perfect!" Nancy agreed. The girls jumped onto the small stage while Ryan located the right disk and adjusted his equipment.

"I need your names," Ryan whispered. They told him their names. He flipped on a spotlight and used a second microphone to introduce Nancy, Bess, and George as River Heights's hottest new trio.

Nancy felt butterflies as she realized that all eyes in the room were on her and her friends.

"Who got us into this, anyway?" George joked to Nancy.

"We can blame Bess if it's a disaster," Nancy said, laughing.

Bess rolled her eyes and took a deep breath. "We'd better get started before I chicken out," she said.

The girls' fears were soon eased by the energetic music. A long keyboard introduction gave them time to relax before having to dive into the lyrics. By the time the first words appeared on the karaoke screen Nancy could feel the audience moving to the rhythm of the popular tune.

Nancy was happy to let Bess lead their singing for the first few bars. Then, gaining confidence that her voice was not going to fail, Nancy moved closer to the mike.

At the end of the first verse George picked up the simple dance step that the real Lavender Dreamers were known for. Nancy and Bess quickly joined in. The music kept them in perfect sync, and the karaoke screen made it easy to remember all the words to the song.

When the last verse was done Nancy raised her hands over her head and started a rhythmic clap that swept over the audience. Soon everyone in the room was clapping with the beat. When the music finally faded out they broke into applause.

"Encore, encore," a voice called from the right of the stage.

Nancy recognized Cami's voice and laughed.

"I've got an idea that will get everybody singing," Nancy said, and she turned to Ryan. "Do you have the song 'Black or White'?" she asked.

"Sure do. I've even memorized the number of the disk it's on," Ryan said.

Nancy quickly explained her plan to George and Bess. "Black or White" was an old Michael Jackson song, but one that everybody in the room would know. She was sure that if she could get the audience to join in, they would be warmed up and ready for karaoke.

With Nancy, George, and Bess on stage leading the action, and Cami striding around the room encouraging the audience, the room was soon filled with clapping and singing.

By the time the music stopped, a line of teenagers stood at the table, eager to pay their money for a chance to sing on stage. Ryan was passing around booklets of song titles.

"That was great," George whispered as they filed off the stage. "I'd even be glad to do another song later."

"So would I," Bess said. "But right now I've got work to do." She hurried back to her chair at the table and smiled at the long line waiting to donate money.

Already another group of girls had stepped onto the stage, smiling nervously.

"We've taken in more than one hundred dollars already," Bess said to Nancy later, when the crowd around the desk finally thinned a bit. "I can't believe it. Finally something's going right."

Two boys dressed in jeans and black T-shirts were performing an old rap favorite as the crowd clapped to the beat. Nancy and George crossed the room to get a better view of the stage.

Suddenly the lights went out and the music stopped.

In the silence that followed Nancy heard Bess shriek, "The money! Someone took the money!"

10

Carson Drew Helps Out

Nancy had only a penlight in her pocket. It shone like a tiny spotlight as she flashed it around the room, across the frightened faces. Then she saw someone racing toward the stairs that were directly to her left.

Nancy instinctively lunged after the fleeing shape, dropping her penlight with a small clatter. As Nancy grabbed hold of the person's shirt she heard a dull thud. But just when she thought she had stopped the thief, she was shoved hard in the chest and knocked to the floor.

She heard screams and shouts as the thief pushed through the crowd and ran down the steps.

Nancy scrambled to her feet just as the lights came back on. She saw George standing by the light switch. Bess stood by the table holding her face in both hands. Cami was searching the floor for the money.

Nancy spotted the money box. It had dropped to the floor when she grabbed the thief. That must have been the thud I heard, she thought.

She picked up the metal box and carried it back to Cami. Then she walked to the corner of the room where Ryan was examining the karaoke machine.

"Did you see anyone?" Nancy asked as she stepped close to Ryan.

"No one. The machine just went dead suddenly," Ryan said. He stepped behind one of the big speakers. A moment later he reappeared, holding the end of a thick cord that had been sliced in two. Nancy's heart sank as she saw the bare copper wires inside.

"I was hoping it had just been unplugged," Ryan said. "Unfortunately, I was wrong. There won't be any more karaoke tonight. I'll have to take this to the shop to get it fixed."

Nancy walked slowly back to the table where Bess was anxiously counting money.

"Thank goodness the box didn't fly open," she said, looking up. "The money's all here."

"But I'm afraid the karaoke machine has been ruined," Nancy said with a sigh.

"Can't we fix it?" Bess asked anxiously.

"The cable's been cut," Nancy said, shaking her head. "There's no way to repair it tonight."

The other teens in the room were already starting to mill around the table and ask when things were going to get going again.

Nancy looked over at Ryan, who was starting to gather up the songbooks. She stepped onto the stage for a second time and held up her hands for quiet. "We have a problem with the karaoke machine," she said, then waited until she had everyone's attention. "I'm sorry, but the fund-raiser is over."

A chorus of sighs and moans rose from the crowd as Nancy stepped off the stage.

Nancy left to call the police. Bess and Cami stood at the table, refunding money to kids who had paid but hadn't yet had their turn to sing.

The crowd was almost gone when Nancy returned. Ryan was carrying his equipment toward the stairs.

"I'm sorry about your machine," Nancy said.

Ryan gave Nancy a weak smile. "Thanks. I'm sorry about your fund-raiser," he said. "Things were looking good for a while."

The girls were alone in the silent room when Sergeant Benson arrived. Nancy filled her in on the attempted theft and the vandalism to the karaoke machine.

"Maybe you girls should stop the fund-raising drive for a while," Sergeant Benson said when she had finished her report. "I'm afraid someone is going to get hurt."

"We can't stop," Bess said, shaking her head. "We have to save the rec center."

Sergeant Benson made some final notes and left the girls alone again.

"If we can't stop whoever is ruining our fund-raisers, there's no way we'll meet our goal by Monday," George said. "I think Nancy is our only hope."

All eyes focused on Nancy. But for once the young detective had no idea how to solve the mystery.

Early the next morning, Thursday, Nancy was on the phone to Chief McGinnis, the River Heights police chief. She hoped that he would know something that would help her.

The police chief said he could meet with her at ten-thirty that morning. Nancy was at his office several minutes early, anxious to get started.

"I'm glad to hear you're working on the fund-raising drive, Nancy," Chief McGinnis said after they shook hands. "The center was always a good place for seniors to gather and for kids to go for safe activities."

"Unfortunately, I'm afraid we're in danger of losing the downtown center permanently," Nancy said, taking a seat opposite him.

"I thought the fund-raising was going quite well," Chief McGinnis said, surprised.

"It was until just a few days ago," Nancy said. "Now someone seems determined to stop us from meeting our goal. And in my investigations I've turned up something else. Now I'm suspicious about the origin of the fire that closed the rec center in the first place."

Nancy explained about finding the unplugged space heater in Mrs. McGregor's old office.

"I'll send an officer back to the River Street center," Chief McGinnis said, frowning. "If the space heater really was unplugged at the time of the fire, we will have to reopen the investigation. With that new evidence we would have to consider arson as a possible cause. Do you have any suspects in mind?"

"I'd like to talk to Nikos Manolotos," Nancy said.

"Yes, he might be able to shed some light on things. Unfortunately, we don't have any good leads as to his whereabouts," Chief McGinnis said. "One of our undercover officers heard he'd gone to Chicago, but then the trail went cold."

"So he could be in River Heights," Nancy said, leaning back in her chair.

"Yes," Chief McGinnis answered. He stood up and paced back and forth behind his chair. "But we've got all our officers looking for him. To stay hidden for so long in this small town, he'd need to have someone bringing food and clothes to him."

"What about Jerry Hartley?" Nancy asked.

"What does he have to do with this?" Chief McGinnis asked, stopping his pacing to face Nancy.

"He's made an offer to buy the rec center," Nancy said. "He's given the board eight days to reply. And there are only six days left."

McGinnis raised his eyebrows and pushed his hands into his pockets. "That is a complication, isn't it?" he said. Then he resumed pacing back and forth behind the chair.

"I've never had any reason to suspect Jerry Hartley of anything," Chief McGinnis said. "He's never been involved in any crimes as far as I know. He's always been supportive of community projects. I have to guess that he's just making a good business offer."

Then the police chief halted his pacing. "Wait—I do remember something," he said. He leafed through the file folders on his desk until he found one labeled Manolotos.

"Here it is," he said. "This was not the first time that Nikos Manolotos was suspected of pocketing fire insurance money."

Nancy raised her eyebrows as she waited for him to finish.

"He was accused of doing the same thing about three years ago," Chief McGinnis said. "The building in that case was the mini-mall next door to the rec center."

"And the owner was Jerry Hartley!" Nancy cried.

"That's right," Chief McGinnis said, smiling at Nancy.

"That makes a connection between Hartley and Manolotos," Nancy said. "Do you think they could be working together?"

"It seems highly unlikely." Chief McGinnis shook his head. "Hartley was the one who brought embezzlement charges against Manolotos the first time. The prosecutor couldn't get enough evidence to go to trial, but Hartley fired Nikos."

"Interesting," Nancy said. "And there's no other connection between them?"

"Not that I'm aware of," McGinnis said.

Nancy paused, cataloging all the facts in her mind. "There are two other suspects, though neither of them is very high on my list," Nancy said. "One is Horace Bell, Mrs. McGregor's friend. He would like to stop the investigation. He says it puts Mrs. McGregor in more danger."

"But does he have a motive for stopping the fund-raising drive?" Chief McGinnis asked, tilting his head to one side.

"Not that I know of," Nancy said. She paused, wondering if there was something about Horace Bell she had missed. Shaking her head, she went on.

"The other suspect is Cory Barnes," she said. "He's a teenager who rides a neon-green skateboard."

"I try to keep up on any problem juveniles, but I haven't heard of Cory," Chief McGinnis said. "Why do you suspect him?"

"Mrs. McGregor banned him from the rec center last spring, so he has a grudge against her. Plus, he seems to be around whenever there is trouble," Nancy explained. "He was at Mrs. McGregor's house after her car was smoke-bombed. Another time we saw him burning signs that were supposed to advertise our car wash. He was also at the karaoke fund-raiser."

"That does sound like a lot of coincidences," the chief said. "I'll ask around about him."

Nancy thanked the chief and left his office.

Nancy checked her watch. It was 11:45. She would have to hurry to pick up Bess and George in time to meet her father for lunch.

George had just finished weighing a load of

aluminum cans when Nancy got to the recycling center. She finished the paperwork quickly, and the girls were on their way.

When Nancy pulled the car up in front of the rec center, Bess was waiting on the sidewalk.

"I thought you'd forgotten me," she said, climbing in the car.

"We couldn't forget you," Nancy said as she drove away. "Especially when we are on our way to lunch."

Putting on an exaggerated pout, Bess pretended to be insulted by Nancy's reference to her love for food. Nancy and George laughed.

When Nancy got to her house her father's car was already in the driveway. Inside the girls could smell a mixture of spices and peanuts mingled with the scent of warm croissants.

"Mmm." Bess threw her head back and closed her eyes as she took in the fragrance. "Mrs. Gruen's been baking."

In the kitchen a basket of flaky croissants sat on the table, and four clear glass plates were piled high with a hearty Oriental chicken salad.

Carson Drew was already seated at the table, catching up on news with Hannah.

Nancy crossed the room and gave her dad a hug from behind his chair. "How was your trip?" she asked.

"Okay, but not very exciting," he said, smiling

at Nancy as the girls sat down. "I'm eager to hear about your case. It must be something big. Hannah says you've been even busier than usual."

"Yes, but not just because of the mystery," Nancy said. "The fund-raising drive is also keeping me busy."

"And the two are intertwined, I bet," Carson Drew said.

"They sure are." Nancy filled her father in on the details of the case.

"You weren't kidding when you said it was the case of the missing suspect," Mr. Drew said. "Not even the police have a clue to where Manolotos is?"

"That's right," Nancy said. "They thought he was in Chicago, but then the trail went cold."

Mr. Drew shook his head and ate his salad slowly. "The name Manolotos sounds so familiar to me," he said. "But I just can't think where I've heard it."

"He was involved in a similar insurance scam once before," George said. "Maybe you remember him from that."

Mr. Drew shook his head again. "I don't think so," he said. "It's something else."

For several minutes the only sound in the kitchen was the clinking of forks on the glass plates as the four ate their lunch.

"I have to tell you, this food is great," Bess said

finally, breaking apart her third croissant. "Hannah Gruen should open a restaurant."

"That's it!" Mr. Drew exclaimed, bringing both hands down on the table. "I remember where I've heard the name Manolotos. And it could mean a break in your case!"

11

Building a Case

The girls all stopped eating and waited for Carson Drew to tell what he knew.

"The Greek Gardens Restaurant in Chicago!" Mr. Drew exclaimed. "About a year ago I was working on a case for a client in Chicago who took me there often. I'm sure the owners were named Manolotos."

"Do you think they could be related to Nikos?" George asked.

"I don't know," Mr. Drew said. "But if the police think that Nikos went to Chicago, it certainly seems worth a try."

"But wouldn't the police already have checked that connection?" Bess asked.

"Not if Manolotos isn't in the Chicago phone

book," Nancy said. "Without knowing that they own the restaurant, the police would have no way of finding Manolotos."

"There's one way to find out," Mr. Drew said.

Nancy pushed her chair back from the table. "I'll call Chief McGinnis right away," she said.

While Nancy made the phone call, Mr. Drew gathered his things.

"The chief's going to check it out," Nancy said as she hung up the receiver.

"That's good. I hope I've helped," Mr. Drew said, looking at his watch. Then, with a quick goodbye, he left to return to his office.

Nancy went to the kitchen, where George and Bess were already helping Hannah clear the table. Hannah excused herself to do some cleaning.

Nancy rinsed plates and silverware and handed them to George, who put them into the dishwasher. Bess wiped off the kitchen table, pushed the chairs in, and then perched herself on the counter.

"Finding Nikos Manolotos would be a great break," Nancy said. "But I can't help feeling that there's something more to this case. I think it's more than coincidence that Nikos used to work for Jerry Hartley."

"But Hartley fired him," George said as she leaned over the dishwasher.

"I know," Nancy said, scrubbing at a plate. "But doesn't it seem strange that Manolotos ended up managing a building that Jerry Hartley wants to buy?"

"And then the building burned," Bess added.

"Exactly," Nancy said, finishing the last dish. "There must be a connection between Manolotos and Hartley. I can feel it."

Nancy wiped the counter clean and sat down. With elbows propped on the table and her chin on her hands she concentrated in silence.

"I see a plan forming," George said as she watched Nancy.

"And something tells me it's going to be dangerous," Bess said with a groan.

"Not if we're careful," Nancy said, sitting up in her chair. "I only want to get inside Jerry Hartley's office building tonight, to have a real look around."

"But there may be night watchmen," Bess said.

"Yes," Nancy said, getting to her feet. "And office cleaners, too." She began digging in one of the kitchen drawers. "We'll each wear one of Hannah's aprons and blend right in," she said. She pulled out a plain blue-and-white bib apron and held it under Bess's chin. She chose similar aprons for herself and George. Each one had two large pockets in the front that could hold cleaning supplies.

The next stop was the laundry room, where Nancy handed bottles of window cleaner, furniture polish, and spot remover to Bess and George. Then she gathered up three dustcloths.

The girls stowed their cleaning supplies and aprons in the trunk of Nancy's car, then drove back to the rec center to help with the car wash and bazaar.

"I sure wish we could find out who recommended Nikos for the manager position," Nancy said as she drove. "Someone must have given him a good word."

"It's too bad there wasn't anything in his personnel file," George said.

With both the car wash and the bazaar going on, the street in front of the rec center was lined with cars. Nancy finally found a place to park. Then she and George helped the Car Wash Kids sponge down cars while Bess collected the money.

When the waiting cars had thinned a bit Nancy and George crossed the street to the rec center.

"It looks as if things are busy here, too," George said as they walked in the front door. Half a dozen people were crowded around the cashier's table, each one waving a piece of merchandise, trying to attract Sammie's attention.

"You look like you could use some help,"

Nancy said to the secretary, stepping behind the desk to join her.

"I sure could," Sammie said, smiling.

Soon George and Nancy were as busy as the secretary, adding up prices, taking money, and making change.

It was almost dark before the crowd started to dwindle. Bess arrived from the car wash and began to count the money collected from the bazaar. Tired volunteers were straightening their craft items on the bazaar tables.

Nancy followed Sammie down to the reception area in the hallway, eyeing the file cabinets in the corner. Her mind drifted back to the mystery.

"Sammie, how do you suppose someone like Nikos Manolotos got the manager's job here?" she asked casually.

"That's easy," the secretary said, straightening some papers on her desk. "He was hired because Stephanie Mann recommended him."

Nancy's jaw dropped. "Are you sure it was Stephanie Mann who recommended him?" Nancy asked Sammie.

"Of course I'm sure," the secretary said. "I'm the one who typed the letter."

"But how did Stephanie Mann know him?" Nancy asked.

The secretary thought for a minute. "I'm afraid

105

my memory isn't that good," she said. "But I remember her asking me to type the letter."

Nancy thanked Sammie for the information and offered to lock up for the night.

When the secretary was gone Nancy and George and Bess got the aprons from Nancy's car. They went back inside the rec center to put on the aprons. Nancy and Bess used the mirror in the rest room to pull their hair back in plain black barrettes.

"I think we look ready for work," Nancy said when they were finished. "Let's go do some cleaning."

They locked and double-checked the doors to the rec center before heading for Nancy's car. It was dark when they rounded the corner at the back of the Hartley Enterprises building.

"I think we're in luck," Nancy said as she drove slowly past the back of the building.

A white pickup truck with a blue top was backing up near the back door of the building, which stood propped open. A man in overalls got out of the truck and walked around to open the tailgate. Lifting out a large toolbox and a stepladder, he disappeared into the building—without closing the back door.

"It looks like the maintenance man is working late," Nancy said. "Just as I'd hoped."

She drove on down the street and parked her car out of sight in an alley.

"Do you really think these disguises will work?" Bess asked as they climbed out of the car.

"If we play our cards right, we may not have to find out," Nancy said. She led the way through the shadows to the side of the Hartley building. The three girls cautiously flattened themselves against the brick wall just around the corner from the back door.

Nancy peeked around the corner. In the dim light she saw the workman come out of the building. He retrieved some more tools from his pickup and disappeared inside again.

"Now," Nancy whispered. Motioning for Bess and George to follow her, she jogged the distance from the corner to the back door. Flattening herself against the wall again, she peeked inside.

The first-floor hallway was empty. To her left was the service elevator. A lighted number above the door told Nancy that the elevator had stopped on the third floor. To her right was a flight of metal stairs.

Nancy motioned her friends to be silent and started up the stairs. When she got to the fifth floor she stopped on the landing. Bess and George stood behind her.

"I wish we could have taken the elevator," Bess said, panting. "That was some climb."

Nancy waited a minute while they all caught their breath. Then she turned the knob on the big metal door and stepped into the fifth-floor hallway. Bess and George followed her.

Nancy let the door close softly behind them. The hallway was dark except for the dim red light of the Exit sign.

The darkness was a good omen, Nancy thought. It meant no one was working on the fifth floor.

Nancy ran her hand along the wall as she moved down the dark hallway. She brushed against the light switch and stopped. Nancy knew she had to make a decision. Real cleaning women would turn on the lights, but that could give away their presence.

Nancy decided to stay with the protection of the darkness. Their disguises seemed good enough, but she would rather go undetected if possible.

The office suite looked different in the darkness. With her penlight Nancy checked the doors until she found the one labeled Earl Gerald Hartley, President. Nancy noted that Hartley went by his middle name. She gave her penlight to George and used a small tool from her pocket to work at the lock.

A moment later the girls were inside. Nancy relocked the door and flicked on the lights.

Bess leaned against the closed office door and let out a long sigh. "Let's hurry and get this done so we can get out of here," she said.

"Good idea," Nancy said. The three girls immediately began looking through drawers in Mr. Hartley's oak desk.

In one bottom drawer Nancy found a few file folders, but there was nothing to connect Jerry Hartley with Nikos Manolotos.

Nancy scanned the designer furniture and modern art arranged around the room. There were no other file cabinets to search. Nancy was beginning to think they had reached another dead end.

Her eyes stopped on a door at the side of the office. Turning the knob, she found that it was unlocked. She opened it up and felt along the wall for a light switch.

The second room was quickly flooded with bright white light. It was a large conference room with a long oak table surrounded by high-backed chairs. On top of the table was an intricate white model of two buildings.

Nancy stepped over to the table for a closer look. Bess and George joined her.

"Look," Nancy said, pointing to the smaller of the two buildings. "This looks like the mini-mall next to the rec center. And there's a skywalk connecting it to this larger building."

"It's an exact duplicate of the mini-mall," said George. "But what does that mean?"

Nancy shook her head. "It means Jerry Hartley isn't planning a parking lot," Nancy said. "He wants the land for a building."

"A big building, too," Bess said, raising her eyebrows.

The second building in the model was much taller than the mini-mall. Nancy quickly counted the windows running up the side.

"Twenty-two stories. That will cost several million dollars," Nancy said, frowning. "And it's been planned for quite a while, I'd guess, if there is a model already."

"But why would he say he wanted the land for a parking lot?" Bess asked.

"Maybe he didn't want anyone to know he's had his eye on that land a long time," Nancy said.

The three girls were still examining the model when they heard a key scratching in the lock of the conference room's hallway door.

"Someone's coming!" Bess whispered in terror.

12

Smoking Out a Criminal

"Quick!" Nancy cried. She grabbed a cleaning cloth and a bottle of furniture polish from the pocket of her apron.

George and Bess followed her lead. When the door opened the three girls were busy polishing the oak table.

A security guard cautiously stepped into the room, his hand on his gun.

"I haven't seen you girls here before," he said suspiciously.

"Of course not," Nancy said, straightening from her work. "We're new."

"Just hired today," George said, still rubbing the wood.

"The hallway light was off when I came up

here," the guard said, still suspicious. "Do you always work in the dark?"

Nancy instantly wished she had made a different decision at the light switch, but she was determined not to let her worry show.

"Not at all," she said. "Someone else must have turned the light off, not realizing we were here."

The security guard stood stone still, watching the girls. He seemed to be considering their story. Nancy was about to give up hope of getting away when the security man smiled and dropped his hand away from his gun.

"Don't work too hard," he said pleasantly. He touched the brim of his hat in a friendly salute and walked back out of the room.

"I thought we were in for it," Bess said when he was gone.

"Me, too," George agreed. "I vote we get out of here fast."

"I won't argue with you on that," Nancy said. "But let's not panic. We could run into that guy again."

The girls turned out the lights, locked the door, and walked back down the hall toward the stairs. This time the hallway was brightly lit. Nancy forced herself to walk casually. She didn't want to look suspicious.

When they got to the landing on the ground

floor, the security guard was walking down the first-floor hallway toward them.

"Finished already?" he asked.

Nancy saw that the look of suspicion had returned to his face.

"All done," she said. "See you in a couple of days." She walked briskly out of the building, with Bess and George close behind.

"I can feel prickles on my back," Bess said as they hurried down the street. "Do you think he'll chase us?"

Nancy looked behind them. The security guard was standing in the doorway of the building. For a moment she thought he might run after them. Then he turned and went back inside.

Nancy, Bess, and George half walked, half jogged back to Nancy's car. After Nancy unlocked the doors Bess collapsed in the backseat. "Take me home," she moaned. "I've had enough detective work for one day!"

Nancy did as Bess asked. But by the time she got to her own front door, Nancy had already formed a plan for the next day.

Just after eight o'clock the next morning Nancy called Mrs. McGregor at her house to set up a meeting. She wanted to talk about her investigation at the Hartley Enterprises building.

"Can you come right now?" Mrs. McGregor asked. "I was going to meet Horace for breakfast, but I can cancel with him. I have to think of the rec center first."

When Nancy arrived at Mrs. McGregor's house half an hour later Horace Bell answered the door. Flip stood obediently by his side.

"Mary says you want to discuss something," he said as soon as Nancy stepped in the door. "I came over as soon as she told me. I hope she's not in more danger."

"Oh, Horace, give the girl some room," Mrs. McGregor said lightly, brushing past Mr. Bell to greet Nancy. "I'm sure she'll tell us everything in due time. Let's all have some doughnuts and herbal tea." She led the way to her cozy kitchen.

Mr. Bell closed his mouth in a stiff frown, pushed his chin out, and followed Mrs. McGregor and Nancy to the kitchen. When Mrs. McGregor had settled into one of the straight-backed chairs Mr. Bell paced the floor behind her.

Nancy told them about the model she had seen in Jerry Hartley's conference room, and about Stephanie Mann having recommended Nikos for the manager's position.

"Do you think Jerry Hartley is behind all the fund-raising problems?" Mrs. McGregor asked Nancy.

"I don't have any proof," Nancy said. "But if he really wants the land badly, he could be trying to stop the rebuilding of the rec center."

"How can I help?" Mrs. McGregor asked, sipping a cup of tea.

"I'd like to set up a meeting with Hartley and convince him we're about to meet our fund-raising goal," Nancy said.

"That will be a long way from the truth," Mrs. McGregor said, setting her cup down. "With all the problems we've had, we're still about five thousand dollars short."

"I know," Nancy said. "But we have to make Jerry Hartley believe that his chance to buy the land is slipping away. Maybe then he'll try something foolish, and we'll get the proof we need to stop him."

"But his something foolish could put Mary in danger," Mr. Bell stormed. "I won't allow this!"

"We'll be careful, Horace," Mrs. McGregor said. "And besides, it may be our only chance to save the rec center." She walked to the phone book, looked up the number for Hartley Enterprises, and began to dial the phone.

Mr. Bell continued to pace, his frown deeper than ever.

"Mr. Hartley, I'd like to meet with you. I have some important news, and . . ." Mrs. McGregor looked at Nancy. She needed a better reason for the call, but she hadn't taken time to think of one.

". . . a plan to help both of us," Nancy whispered.

Mrs. McGregor smiled and repeated the words to Jerry Hartley.

Nancy was impressed by Mrs. McGregor's calm, convincing voice.

"Yes, that will be fine," Mrs. McGregor said, then put the receiver back in its place.

"He'll see us at two o'clock," she said with a smile. "At his office."

Nancy used the rest of the morning to help George at the recycling center. After a quick lunch she met Mrs. McGregor at the Hartley Enterprises building.

Nancy wasn't at all surprised that Jerry Hartley greeted her with a smile, just as he had the day she and George had visited. She decided against asking him about his involvement with Nikos Manolotos. She didn't want him to know she was investigating. Their plan would never work if he was suspicious.

"It's nice to see you again, Ms. Drew," Hartley said as he shook Nancy's hand. "And nice to meet you, Mrs. McGregor. Now what's this wonderful plan you have to help us both out?"

Mrs. McGregor smiled warmly. "First I'd like to tell you that we're very near our fund-raising goal," she said, taking a chair opposite Hartley's desk.

Nancy watched Hartley's reaction closely. He only smiled.

"Why, that is good news," he said. "Of course, my plans will change, but I suppose I could buy the vacant lot instead."

"I'm happy to see you aren't too disappointed," Mrs. McGregor said. "We want the rec center to be on friendly terms with its neighbors. That's why we came up with a plan for a parking lot."

"A parking lot for the River Street Recreation Center?" Mr. Hartley asked, looking confused.

"Well, we will need additional parking when the center gets rebuilt." Mrs. McGregor delivered her story carefully. "But most of our classes are in the evening, after your mini-mall closes. So we thought maybe we could share the parking lot. The rec center could contribute toward the cost of upkeep."

Nancy saw no negative reaction from Hartley. His smile only broadened.

"It sounds like a good idea," he said. "Of course, we'll have to discuss it further—after I purchase the property."

"And after we get our new building finished," Mrs. McGregor said.

"Splendid," Hartley said, opening the center drawer of his desk. "Now, how close did you say you were to your goal?"

Mrs. McGregor raised her eyebrows. That was one question she hadn't been ready for.

"We're only three hundred dollars away," Nancy improvised. "And we still have the weekend to finish up."

"That surprises me," Hartley said evenly. "Yesterday the total on your thermometer was much lower. I noticed it when I was at the mini-mall."

"We've been so busy raising money we haven't had time to change the sign," Nancy said brightly.

"To show there are no hard feelings, let me help you reach the goal," Hartley said. He pulled a large green checkbook from his desk. Nancy watched in disbelief as Hartley made out a check and handed it to Mrs. McGregor.

"I'm looking forward to talking to you about the parking lot again later," he said as Nancy and Mrs. McGregor stood up to leave. "Now let me walk you to the elevator."

As they walked down the hall Nancy noticed that the door to the conference room was open.

"That's an impressive model," Nancy said,

pretending to see the model of the buildings for the first time.

"Yes, the architects did a nice job on it," Hartley agreed.

"That looks like your mini-mall on the right," Nancy said, stopping by the open door.

"It does, doesn't it?" Jerry Hartley said pleasantly. "It's actually a building in Chicago."

"What a coincidence that they look so much alike," Nancy said, watching Hartley's face.

"Not really," Mr. Hartley said. "They were both built at the same time by my father's construction company."

Nancy felt she had struck out again. There was nothing more to do but follow Jerry Hartley down the hall to the elevators. Once inside, Mrs. McGregor handed Nancy the check.

"One hundred dollars," Nancy said, holding it in front of her. "Not a bad donation."

"No," Mrs. McGregor said. "And not what I'd expect from someone who wanted to tear down the rec center."

"I guess I really misjudged him." Nancy sighed. "Now I'm back to square one. This is one of the most baffling mysteries I've ever had."

The drive back to the rec center was a quiet one. Nancy was at a dead end. Hartley seemed not to be involved after all, and there was still no clue as to where Nikos might be.

"I guess it's back to work," Mrs. McGregor said when they pulled up in front of the rec center. "Now that we've said we're almost to our goal, we'll have to try to make it true."

Nancy followed Mrs. McGregor inside.

"There's a message for you, Nancy," Sammie called when Nancy walked in the door. "Chief McGinnis would like you to call him right away. You can use my phone."

Nancy dialed the phone and asked for the chief. "I hope you have some news," she said to him. "I seem to be running into a blank wall at every turn."

"Every turn but one," the chief said. "The lead you had in Chicago panned out. Our police contacts in Chicago did find the Manolotos family there, and they do have a son named Nikos."

"Do they know where he is?" Nancy asked hopefully.

"No, they said they hadn't talked to him for several months," the chief said. "The officer in Chicago was convinced they were telling the truth."

"So it *was* another dead end," Nancy said.

"Not quite. It seems the Manolotos family includes a daughter who lives in River Heights." The chief paused. "Her name is Stephanie."

Nancy's mouth dropped open as she considered this new information. It could mean only one thing. "Is Nikos's sister Stephanie Mann?" she asked the chief.

She cast a glance at Mrs. McGregor, who couldn't help overhearing. Mrs. McGregor gasped in astonishment.

"One and the same," Chief McGinnis said. "I checked the records myself. Stephanie Mann used to be Stephanie Manolotos. She had her name legally shortened about five years ago."

"Do you suppose she was planning a political career even then?" Nancy asked.

"That would be my guess," Chief McGinnis said. "She probably felt Mann would be an easier name for voters to remember than Manolotos."

"Plus it would help her avoid any connection with her unethical brother," Nancy added. "Do you think she knows where Nikos is?"

"If she does, she's not admitting it," Chief McGinnis said. "I already had an officer question her. She said she hasn't heard from him since the fire."

As Nancy hung up she wondered if Stephanie had another reason for being at Nikos's house the other night. Stephanie Mann obviously had hidden her relationship with her brother very carefully. How far would the politician go to keep it a secret from the public?

"I can't believe Stephanie Mann is Nikos's sister," Mrs. McGregor said, raising her eyebrows. "So that's why she recommended him for the manager's job! Do you suppose she's also hiding him?"

"I don't know, but there may be a way to find out," Nancy said, reaching for the phone book. "I've got an idea for my own kind of smoke bomb. Maybe we can spook Stephanie into leading us to Nikos."

13

One Piece of the Puzzle

"I hope you're not calling to ask for an extension of the fund-raising deadline," Stephanie said when Nancy introduced herself on the phone.

"Why, no," Nancy said. "Actually, I'm looking forward to the next board meeting—Ms. Manolotos."

Nancy waited. There was a short silence, and then Stephanie whispered, "How did you find out?"

"Let's just say I have my sources," Nancy said. "And tomorrow morning I'm going to call the rest of the board members. I'll tell them you recommended your own brother for the job of manager—even though you knew he'd been suspected of stealing insurance money before."

Again there was silence. "What do I have to do to keep you quiet?" Stephanie said at last.

"There's only one thing that would change my mind," Nancy said. "Nikos has to give himself up. I'll wait until ten o'clock tomorrow morning."

There was a pause and then a click on the other end of the line.

"I haven't got a moment to lose," Nancy said to Mrs. McGregor, hanging up the phone. "I must go find George and Bess. We've got work to do."

"You girls be careful," Mrs. McGregor said anxiously.

Nancy stopped. What if Nikos decided to seek revenge instead of giving himself up? she thought. Mrs. McGregor could still be a target, since she had pushed the police to bring him to justice.

"It might be best if you're not at your house tonight, Mrs. McGregor," Nancy suggested gently.

Mrs. McGregor looked deep into Nancy's eyes and then let out a long sigh.

"All right—I'll go to Horace's for the evening," she said. "But only until eleven o'clock. Then I'm going home, Nikos or no Nikos."

"Thanks," Nancy said. "I'll call you at Mr. Bell's if it's safe before then."

Nancy ran across the street to the car wash to

get Bess. Cami agreed to collect the money so that Bess could go with Nancy.

Then the two teens drove to the recycling center, where George was working. After they explained the latest developments to George, she raced through her paperwork and left with them.

Nancy drove her two friends back to her house. They made some quick sandwiches and grabbed a bunch of Hannah's freshly baked cookies. Nancy jotted down Stephanie Mann's address from the phone book. Then they headed toward her house.

It was dark when Nancy pulled her car to a stop a half block from Stephanie Mann's. She was pleased to see Ms. Mann's white convertible parked down the street. That meant Stephanie was probably still at home. Nancy parked between two other cars where she was sure she wouldn't be noticed.

"Do you really think that threat will scare her into going to Nikos?" Bess asked.

"If it doesn't, we've got a long night ahead of us," Nancy said, pulling one of the sandwiches from the brown paper bag. "Better make yourselves comfortable."

Bess was licking cookie crumbs off her fingers when Nancy motioned for silence and leaned forward in her seat. Down the street the lights went off one by one in Stephanie's house. A dark figure came out the front door and hurried to the convertible.

"That's got to be Stephanie," George said as the car pulled away from the curb.

Nancy started the engine of her own car and followed cautiously behind Stephanie Mann. They wound through the streets of the middle-class residential district and into an area of run-down apartments and small, unkempt houses.

Stephanie's white convertible and Nancy's blue sports car were the only vehicles on the street. Nancy dropped more than a block behind, but she was sure Stephanie would notice her at any moment. To her relief, Stephanie pulled her car over to the curb in front of an old apartment building and stopped.

Nancy parked half a block away.

"I don't like this place," Bess said. "Can't we call the police and let them handle it?"

"Not until we know what apartment he's in," Nancy said. She slipped out of the car and tossed her keys to George. "If I'm not back in ten minutes, call the police."

Nancy jogged the half block to the run-down apartment building. She ran up the front steps two at a time.

Inside, the empty hallway was dimly lit. Papers and soda cans littered the floor. The doors on

126

both sides of the hallway were battered and unpainted. Some had dented metal numbers on them, some had only the faded stains where numbers had been.

Nancy listened carefully at each door, but none of the voices she heard sounded like Stephanie Mann's.

At the end of the hallway a dirty stairway led to the second floor. The steps creaked as Nancy climbed them.

At the top she stopped and listened again. Faintly, from down the hall, Nancy heard yelling. She crept forward until she could clearly hear Stephanie's voice coming from one of the rooms.

"You have to turn yourself in," Stephanie said. "I'll lend you money. You can give back what you stole."

Nancy heard a deep, vicious laugh come from the apartment. "That will hardly be enough now, Sis," the voice said. "The building's already burned down. I'll be sued for the loss."

Nancy knew she had finally found Nikos Manolotos. She leaned closer to the door to catch the rest of the conversation.

"I'm still the chairwoman," Stephanie said, her voice lower. "I'll tell them it was all a terrible mistake—that you didn't mean for anything bad to happen."

"But you'd be wrong," Nikos said. His menacing voice was so low that Nancy could barely hear him.

"What do you mean?" Stephanie asked, her voice wavering.

"I set that fire," Nikos said. "I burned the building on purpose."

"But why?" Stephanie begged.

Nancy could hear Nikos start to answer, but his voice was too quiet. She was sure he was about to give away the solution to this mystery, if she could only hear!

Carefully Nancy turned the knob and pushed the door open just an inch. As she did the door creaked ever so slightly.

Nikos jerked around and pulled the door open.

Nancy was facing a dark, angry man at least a foot taller than herself. She saw Nikos grab a heavy glass vase from a small end table beside him. His face was twisted in a menacing sneer.

"Excuse me, I must have the wrong apartment," Nancy said quickly. She took a step backward, pulling the door toward her.

Nikos lunged forward.

As soon as he was close to her, Nancy shoved the door open again with all her strength. It hit Nikos in the face, sending him staggering. The vase went flying and shattered on the floor. He was still off balance when Nancy hit him in the stomach with a sharp karate kick.

Nikos doubled over. Nancy hit him on the back of the neck with her open hand. He fell to the floor with a thud.

Nancy was on top of him in an instant. She grabbed a telephone and wrapped the cord tightly around Nikos's hands. As she did she silently hoped that George was already calling the police.

Stephanie had fallen to her knees on the wooden floor. Tears were streaming down her cheeks.

Nancy looked around the apartment for something to tie Nikos's feet. "Bring me the sheet off the bed," Nancy said to the sobbing Stephanie.

Stephanie reacted slowly.

"Quickly!" Nancy ordered. "Before he comes to!"

Stephanie struggled to her feet and staggered across the room to the bed. She yanked hard at the sheet until it finally came loose. She handed it to Nancy, who used it to bind Nikos's feet.

"That should hold him until the police come," Nancy said to Stephanie. "Did he tell you why he set the fire?"

Stephanie was sitting on the bed, her head in her hands. "No," she sobbed. "He only told me I knew too much. I'm so sorry all this happened. I just wanted to protect him."

And protect your own reputation, Nancy thought. She felt sorry for Stephanie, but at the

129

same time the politician was partly responsible for all that had happened. She was the one who had recommended Nikos for the manager's job. And after the disastrous fire she had hidden her guilty brother from the police.

"Did you help him with the smoke bombs and the threatening letters?" Nancy asked.

Stephanie lifted her face, and her eyes met Nancy's. "No. I only helped him hide. I wouldn't even have done that if I'd known he set the fire," she declared. "I only knew he took the money. I wanted to protect him."

"And what about the night I saw you at Nikos's house?" Nancy asked.

"Like I told you that night, I was looking for evidence to clear myself," Stephanie said, turning her eyes back to the floor. "But I was also getting clothes for Nikos. When I saw you through the window I panicked. I was scared someone would find out I was hiding him."

"And your trying to sell the rec center—is Nikos behind that, too?" Nancy asked.

"We agreed on that," Stephanie said, looking up. "I thought if the rec center was rebuilt someplace else, maybe it would all blow over. I just wanted people to forget what Nikos had done."

"You'd better tell all this to the police when they arrive," Nancy said. She turned to Nikos, who was beginning to moan softly. He rolled over on the floor and struggled to a sitting position.

"And if you're smart, you'll be prepared to talk, too," Nancy told him. "The police will want to know why you set the fire and who your partner is."

Nikos looked at her defiantly. "I'm not telling you or the police anything," he said. "And you don't have any evidence on me except for the insurance scam. I probably won't even get jail time for that."

Nancy knew he was right. She had heard his confession, but without hard evidence it wouldn't be enough for a conviction.

"We have proof that you sent those threats to Mary McGregor," Nancy said, hoping she could bluff him into giving her more information. "And that you planted the smoke bombs in her car and at the rec center."

Nikos snorted. "I'd never be stupid enough to write a threatening letter," he said. "Only a fool would do something that could show up in court. And if I set a bomb, it would be more than smoke."

Nancy had the eerie feeling he was telling the truth. That meant there was someone else involved. She was sure it wasn't Stephanie. That left Cory Barnes, Horace Bell, and Jerry Hartley as possible suspects.

"Maybe you didn't write the letters, but apparently your partner did," Nancy said, still bluffing. "And when we catch him, I bet he won't protect you. If you're smart, you'll help us now."

"Even if I did have a partner, I wouldn't tell you or anyone else," Nikos said.

Nancy thought, trying to come up with a next move. The silence was broken by the sound of police sirens growing ever closer.

"Why don't you tell me who your partner is now?" she said. "It will be better for you in the end if we can save the rec center."

Nikos's wicked laugh filled the room. Nancy glanced at Stephanie.

"I'd tell you if I knew." Stephanie shrugged. "I don't want to protect him any longer."

Nikos was silent as Chief McGinnis and several officers came through the open door of the apartment. Bess and George were right behind them.

"Thank goodness you're all right," Bess said to Nancy. "When you didn't come out in ten minutes we called the police from a phone booth. We were sure something had happened."

"And you were right," Chief McGinnis said. "Something certainly has happened. But as usual, Nancy came out on top." He clapped Nancy on the shoulder.

"Meet Nikos Manolotos," Nancy said to the chief. "He's confessed to setting the rec center fire and stealing the insurance money. But I'm sure he has a partner, and he won't say who it is."

Nancy told Chief McGinnis what Nikos and Stephanie had said and done before he arrived.

When Nancy had finished her report she walked back to her car with Bess and George. "I guess we'd better go tell Mrs. McGregor what's happened," Bess said.

"If only finding Nikos had provided a more complete solution to the mystery," Nancy said as she drove away. "I was hoping we could tell Mrs. McGregor that everything was resolved."

"Maybe something will turn up," George said as they drove through the deserted streets. "At least half a solution is better than none."

It was almost nine o'clock when Nancy, Bess, and George got back to Mr. Bell's house. Mr. Bell answered the door with his usual frown.

"Did you catch him?" he demanded immediately. "Did you catch Nikos Manolotos?"

"Yes, but the police don't have much evidence," Bess said. "Nancy thinks he has a partner, but Nikos isn't talking."

"Then you've just stirred things up," Mr. Bell said. "I told you to stay out of this."

"Is Nikos in jail?" Mrs. McGregor asked, motioning for the girls to come in.

Bess began to tell the story, but then the telephone rang. Mr. Bell went to answer it. After saying a few words he opened a drawer in the small stand and took out a notepad and pencil.

Mrs. McGregor waved the girls toward the kitchen. "Help me get some soft drinks," she said.

Mrs. McGregor got glasses, and Nancy went to the freezer for ice cubes. Bess sat at the kitchen table and began again to tell about the capture of Nikos and Stephanie.

Nancy reached into the plastic bin and grabbed a handful of ice. She dumped four cubes into one of the tall glasses Mrs. McGregor held out. Then she reached back into the freezer.

Her hand touched something strange. It was cold and smooth like an ice cube, but the wrong shape. Nancy closed her fingers around it and pulled it out of the freezer.

It was a small silver lighter, the kind her grandfather had used to light his pipe. Nancy looked at it and flipped it over.

On the back were the initials EGH.

Nancy felt her heart jump. EGH could be Earl Gerald Hartley's initials. But what was his lighter doing in Horace Bell's house? And why was it hidden in the ice cube bin?

14

The Mystery Heats Up

Grasping the lighter, Nancy looked through the open doorway toward the telephone. Horace Bell still held the receiver, but he was staring at Nancy's hand, his face ash white. The piece of notepaper he was holding was crushed as his hand closed into a tense fist.

Horace walked slowly to the kitchen, still staring at Nancy's hand. His mouth was open, but no words came out.

"These are Jerry Hartley's initials," Nancy said, holding out the lighter. She was aware that everyone was staring at Horace Bell. He was speechless.

"Horace," Mrs. McGregor said, breaking the stunned silence, "what does this mean? Are you involved with Jerry Hartley?"

"I—I—" Mr. Bell stammered as he reached for the back of a kitchen chair to steady himself. "Certainly not," he finally said after taking a deep breath. He dropped heavily into the chair. Mrs. McGregor, Nancy, Bess, and George stood stone still, waiting for him to explain.

Staring at the blank wall of the kitchen, Mr. Bell spoke in a weak voice. "I found the lighter at the rec center the morning of the fire," he said.

Mrs. McGregor, Nancy, and George quickly sat down in the other three chairs around the small table. Bess pulled up a wooden stool from the corner and crowded in between Mrs. McGregor and Nancy. All eyes were on Horace.

"I was walking Flip along the nature trail just as the sun came up," Mr. Bell began. His hands relaxed in front of him as he started to talk. The crumpled piece of notepaper fell on the table.

"When we passed behind the rec center I thought I smelled smoke, so I left the trail for a closer look," he recalled. "The back door was open a crack, and I went in. I smelled the smoke again, and I heard voices coming from Mary's office. Flip and I went down the hall to look."

Mr. Bell stopped and began to play with the paper in front of him.

"Go on, Horace," Mrs. McGregor said, reaching across the table to put her hand on his arm.

Her voice was firm but gentle. Her eyes were focused on his face. "What did you find?"

Nancy folded her arms on the table in front of her. She could see concern in Mrs. McGregor's eyes—and confusion, as though she wasn't sure whether to comfort Mr. Bell or be angry.

"There was a fire in front of the space heater," he went on. "Two men were stacking papers on the fire to make the blaze bigger. One of them was Nikos—I'd seen him at the center before, so I knew him. I didn't recognize the other man.

"About that time Flip growled, and they turned around and saw us." Horace swallowed hard and continued. "Nikos recognized me from times I've been there with Mary. . . . She always kept a picture of me on her desk."

Mr. Bell stopped and looked up at Mrs. McGregor. Nancy thought she saw a tear begin to form at the corner of his eye.

"Nikos picked up the picture. He slammed the frame against the desk, breaking the glass. Then he put the picture on the flames and laughed while it burned," Mr. Bell said, still looking at Mrs. McGregor. "He said he'd hurt you, Mary, if I told anyone! I know he meant it. I couldn't let that happen."

Mrs. McGregor pulled a handkerchief from the pocket of her cotton pants and dabbed her eyes slowly.

Mr. Bell looked back at the crumpled paper and shook his head. "I tried to stop them," he said, his voice quiet, "but Nikos hit me. He must have knocked me out, because the next thing I remember was Flip licking my face. I was lying on the floor, and the office was filled with smoke. The fire was already burning up the wall.

"I started to get up, and my hand hit that lighter. I knew it must have been what they used to start the fire. I grabbed it, and then Flip and I got out."

"Was the other man Jerry Hartley?" Nancy asked gently.

Mr. Bell shook his head. "I never knew," he said. "Later that day I got a phone call saying Mary would be hurt if I talked. I guessed it was from the second man, but I didn't know who he was.

"I knew I should give the lighter to the police," he said sheepishly, looking up at Nancy. "But I couldn't put Mary at risk, so I hid it. I thought maybe someday I could turn it in."

"What did the second man look like?" Nancy asked.

"He wasn't quite as tall as me," Mr. Bell said. "But heavier, almost fat. He had wavy hair—brown, I think."

"That sounds like Jerry Hartley," George said to Nancy.

"Oh, Horace, you should have told me. We could have helped each other," Mrs. McGregor said, reaching across the table to take Mr. Bell's hand. "I can't bear the thought of you lying in that burning building. You're lucky you weren't killed!"

Meanwhile Nancy's eyes were on the note Mr. Bell had dropped on the table.

"May I see that?" she asked.

Mr. Bell handed the paper to her. "It's a phone message for Mary," he said.

Nancy wasn't looking at the writing. It was the yellow paper that interested her. There was nothing unusual about the size or shape, and even the color was fairly common. But it was the same color as the threatening notes they had found in the magazine at the recycling center and in Mrs. McGregor's office.

"Did you send the threatening notes?" Nancy asked cautiously. She didn't want to make either Mr. Bell or Mrs. McGregor angry.

Mr. Bell met her eyes. "I did," he confessed. Nancy saw his lip start to quiver. He raised his hand to his face to cover his mouth.

Nancy couldn't help but feel sorry for the elderly man. Now she knew the reason for his constant irritable frown—he had been genuinely frightened that Mary McGregor would be hurt.

Mrs. McGregor handed Mr. Bell her handkerchief as a tear ran down his face. He took it and dabbed his cheek.

"I only wanted to keep Mary safe," he apologized, looking at his friend and then back at Nancy. "I couldn't tell her what I'd seen— Manolotos and Hartley would have hurt her for sure if I had. But I thought she might back off from the search for Nikos if she felt she was in danger. So I slipped the first note under her door. I put the second one on her desk when she was at the board meeting. I never guessed there would be a smoke bomb there the same day, or that Nancy would catch me walking behind the rec center."

Then Mr. Bell's voice turned angry. "Mary's house being ransacked, and the smoke bombs—I knew what those meant," he said. "Hartley was just telling me in his own cruel way that he really could hurt Mary whenever he wanted to."

Now that Nancy finally understood what Mr. Bell had been through she could see why he had been so overprotective of Mrs. McGregor. The gentle look in the elderly woman's eye told Nancy that Mrs. McGregor understood, too.

Nancy handed Mrs. McGregor the phone message. Reading the note, Mrs. McGregor frowned. "I don't recognize this number, Horace," she said. "Who was it?"

"He said he was a neighbor," Mr. Bell answered. "He said he wanted to be sure you were okay, since he'd noticed you hadn't come home. I said you were here and that you were safe. I was surprised he didn't want to talk to you, but I took his number in case you wanted to call back."

Nancy was instantly alert. "Someone was making sure Mrs. McGregor was here?" she said, jumping to her feet.

She took the message and rushed to the phone. Quickly she dialed the number Mr. Bell had written down.

"Jake's Quick Serve," the woman's voice on the other end of the line said.

"Did someone borrow your phone a few minutes ago?" she asked.

"Yeah. The pay phone's broken, so I let him use it," the woman said. "He's gone now, though."

Nancy asked what the man had looked like. Just as Nancy feared, the woman described Jerry Hartley.

Nancy put the phone down slowly. She looked around the kitchen, sensing danger. She saw Flip standing by the back door, his hair bristling.

"Stay here," Nancy said to Mrs. McGregor as she started out of the kitchen. "And don't open the door for anyone. I'm going to have a look around."

"We'll come with you," George said, getting to her feet and tugging at Bess's sleeve.

"Right," Bess said reluctantly.

The three of them walked quickly through the living room and out the front door. It took Nancy only a moment to spot the gray van half a block down the street. Nancy began to jog toward it with Bess and George behind her.

They had covered about half the distance when a dark figure cut through a yard in front of them and jumped into the van. With tires squealing, the van lurched away from the curb and careened down the street.

When Nancy turned back toward Horace's house, smoke was billowing up from the rear of it. Moments later orange flames were licking skyward.

"Oh, no!" Bess screamed. "The house is on fire! Mrs. McGregor and Mr. Bell are inside!"

15

A Newfound Courage

Nancy knew she would have to act fast to save Horace and Mary. "George, find a neighbor to call the fire department," she yelled.

George was sprinting to the nearest house even before Nancy had finished.

Nancy and Bess hurried back to the front door. When Nancy opened it she could see that the living room was already filled with smoke. She bent down, trying to stay low as she went toward the kitchen, where she had last seen Mrs. McGregor and Mr. Bell.

"Mrs. McG!" Bess called from behind Nancy.

From ahead of them Nancy heard coughing and then Mr. Bell's voice.

"Over here," he said.

Nancy moved toward the sound. She finally

caught sight of Mr. Bell through the dense smoke. He had pulled Mrs. McGregor's arm over his shoulders and was half dragging her toward the door.

Nancy quickly stepped under Mrs. McGregor's other arm. Together they were able to get Mrs. McGregor out of the burning house and into the fresh evening air.

"The fire department and the police are on their way," George said as she ran back across the lawn toward them.

"Flip!" Mr. Bell yelled. "Where's Flip?" He had put Mrs. McGregor down on the grass and was heading back toward the house. "I have to save my dog!"

Nancy knew it was foolish to go back into a burning building after a dog, but she wondered if she would be able to keep Mr. Bell from doing it.

"Flip!" Mr. Bell called again from the doorway.

Just as he was about to dive into the billowing smoke for the second time, the small brown-and-white dog leapt from the smoke into Mr. Bell's arms.

"You little rascal," Mr. Bell said, laughing wildly in relief. He carried the squirming dog down the steps and put him down beside Mrs. McGregor. Mr. Bell sat down, too, and put his arms around Mrs. McGregor. "Thank goodness we're all safe," he said.

A moment later two fire engines roared to a halt in front of the small wooden house. Fire fighters began racing across the lawn with hoses. Soon heavy streams of water were aimed at the house.

Mrs. McGregor, Mr. Bell, Nancy, George, and Bess hurried out of the fire fighters' way. They were standing next to the curb when Chief McGinnis parked his police car and got out.

"I came as soon as I heard it was George who called," Chief McGinnis said. "I had two other squad cars help me check out the neighborhood. I told them to watch for a gray van. Guess what they came up with?"

"I'd bet it was Jerry Hartley with a can of gasoline," Nancy said, cocking her head to one side. "My guess is he decided we knew too much. When he found us all in one house he made his move."

"Right as usual," the chief said. "Hartley also had some military smoke bombs in his van. We'll learn more when we question him."

"Before you do, look in the Hartley Enterprises building for a model of a shopping center," Nancy said. "Hartley said it was going to be built in Chicago, but I'm sure you'll find that was a lie. He was planning to put it right where the rec center is now. But first he had to get his hands on the property. His plan to do that started with burning the building."

"Nancy, you're a smart detective," Chief McGinnis said, folding his arms. "But I don't know how we're ever going to prove he started the rec center fire."

Nancy turned and saw Mr. Bell silhouetted against the flames of the burning house. He had his arm around Mrs. McGregor, and Flip sat beside them on the grass. The three were watching the fire fighters pour water on Mr. Bell's home.

"I don't think you'll have any trouble proving that," Nancy said. "You've got an eyewitness to the arson. Horace Bell saw the whole thing. After tonight I think he'll be more than ready to testify."

"Well, I'll be," Chief McGinnis said as he stepped back to his squad car. He pulled out a notebook and pen and walked over to talk to Horace Bell.

The River Street rec center meeting room was decorated with purple and silver streamers for the big fund-raising dinner on Saturday night. A net on the ceiling held matching balloons.

When Nancy, George, and Bess arrived they saw Cami standing behind a chair at the head table, beaming as she helped Mrs. McGregor greet guests.

"Nice job on the decorations," Bess said when they reached Mrs. McGregor. "I love the colors."

"Thanks," Mrs. McGregor said. "Cami and the Car Wash Kids helped me blow up the balloons. Even Cory helped! I wanted tonight to be special."

"I'm sure it will be," Bess said. "And I hope they start serving dinner soon. With Hannah Gruen and a dozen of the best cooks in River Heights acting as chefs, the food should be as great as the decorations."

Nancy and George laughed.

"Count on Bess to know the details about the food," Nancy said.

It didn't take the girls long to find their place cards. They were all seated at the head table. Nancy was on one side of Chief McGinnis, and Bess and George on the other.

A dozen boys and girls began carrying plates of hot food to the guests. Nancy recognized Cory Barnes among the servers.

Cory smiled as he set a plate of spinach salad and roast turkey at each place at the head table.

"I'm glad you saved the rec center," he said to Nancy. "It really is a fun place. And Mrs. McGregor isn't so bad."

Nancy smiled back. She was glad Cory Barnes

147

had turned out to be innocent. Maybe she'd see him in karate class next summer, she thought.

As they were enjoying dessert they heard the clink of metal on glass. They looked up to see Mary McGregor tapping her water glass with a butter knife.

"Mrs. McGregor is going to make a great chairwoman of the board of directors," Bess whispered. "I'm so glad the board named her to replace Stephanie."

Nancy smiled. Mrs. McGregor had been the obvious choice to head the board when the emergency board meeting was held that afternoon. The board had acted quickly after Stephanie Mann was arrested for hiding a criminal.

At the same meeting they had voted unanimously not to sell the rec center. That was hardly a surprise, since Jerry Hartley was no longer in a position to buy it.

"I'd like to thank each of you for coming," Mrs. McGregor told the crowd when everyone had quieted down. "And I want to thank Nancy Drew for giving us time to finish our fund-raising drive. I think we can reach our ten-thousand-dollar goal in two weeks or less."

Mrs. McGregor's prediction was met by enthusiastic applause.

Nancy turned to Chief McGinnis. "So what did you finally learn from Jerry Hartley?" she asked.

"Thanks to your detective work, we had enough evidence to get both Hartley and Nikos to talk," Chief McGinnis said between bites of chocolate cake. "Nikos said it was Hartley's idea that he apply for the manager's job. Hartley agreed to drop the earlier embezzlement charges and promised him ten thousand dollars if he would steal the insurance money.

"Nikos convinced Stephanie he wanted to go straight and pressured her for the job recommendation," the chief continued. "He had to make sure there was no insurance when he burned the building down. Otherwise it would be too easy to rebuild."

"And it all started to go wrong when Mr. Bell saw them setting the fire," Bess said as she scooped up a forkful of fudge icing.

"That's right. Hartley was so scared that Horace would spill the beans that he started his campaign to terrorize Mary McGregor just to keep Horace in line," Chief McGinnis said. "He ransacked Mary's house and planted the smoke bombs in her car and at the rec center. Then Hartley called Horace and threatened to do worse things if Horace told anyone what he'd seen."

"Did Nikos have anything to do with those threats?" Nancy asked.

"Apparently not," Chief McGinnis said. "Nikos went into hiding immediately and was pretty much out of the picture after the fire. But he did pressure Stephanie to support selling the property. He was hoping for a quick sale so he could get his money from Hartley and get out of town."

"Hartley didn't count on Mrs. McG starting the fund-raising drive," Bess said.

"That's right," the chief said. "When the fund-raising looked like it was going to be successful Hartley stepped up his activities. The sabotaged crusher at the recycling center was his handiwork. So was the trouble at the karaoke night. And he also burned the car wash signs."

"To think I had my hands on him," Nancy said, remembering the struggle in the dark at karaoke night. "If only I'd been able to hold on."

"At least you saved the money," Bess said.

"Did Hartley admit to starting the fire at Mr. Bell's house?" Nancy asked.

"Yes, we pretty much had him cold on that. We even got the clerk at Jake's Quick Serve to identify him as the man who made the phone call," Chief McGinnis said.

"I'm sure he didn't plan to leave that phone

number," Nancy said. "It's a good thing Mr. Bell pressured him for it."

"And a good thing you figured out what the call was really about," Chief McGinnis said. "Hartley only made it to find out where Mrs. McGregor was. He panicked when she convinced him that the fund-raising was nearly successful. He wanted her out of the way, and fast, so that he could still have a shot at buying the property.

"When he got there and saw your car, Nancy," the chief added, "he couldn't resist trying to get rid of all his problems at once."

"What about the plumbing van?" George asked. "Does Hartley really have a plumbing business?"

"No. He just painted the word 'Plumbing' on his van so he wouldn't look suspicious parking on residential streets," McGinnis said, wiping his lips with a napkin.

"And it almost worked," Nancy said. "Has Stephanie been charged with a crime?"

Chief McGinnis took a sip of coffee. "She's charged with aiding and abetting a criminal for her part in hiding Nikos," the chief said. "But she may get off with a fine and some community service. Nikos and Hartley are both charged with arson, fraud, and several other crimes. I'm sure we'll be able to keep them behind bars for a long time."

151

"What about Mr. Bell?" Bess asked quietly.

"Well, we can't charge him for the threats," the chief said with a laugh. "Mary refuses to press charges. She says he was just trying to protect her, and that she wasn't scared anyway, so it shouldn't matter."

"That sounds like Mrs. McG," Bess said. "Hartley and Manolotos tangled with the wrong woman when they tangled with her."

"But what about the other charges?" Nancy asked.

"Horace will be charged for withholding evidence," McGinnis said, "but I doubt he'll go to jail—especially with Mary McGregor fighting for him. She's already told me I should leave him alone."

"Horace Bell is lucky to have a friend like Mary McGregor," Bess said.

"And I'm lucky to have a friend like Horace Bell," Mrs. McGregor said from behind the girls.

Nancy turned around and saw Mrs. McGregor and Mr. Bell holding hands.

"Remember, he saved my life," Mrs. McGregor said. "And when he's not trying to protect me from every little thing, he's quite a wonderful friend."

Nancy could see that Mr. Bell's neck had stiffened again, but then a smile crept over his lips. For the first time since the mystery began Nancy saw Horace Bell's eyes twinkle.

"And with Nancy Drew as my witness," he said, "I promise not to be overprotective ever again—unless someone tries to hurt my Mary."

"Horace, you're impossible," Mrs. McGregor said, slapping his shoulder gently.

Mr. Bell pretended not to notice and leaned over Nancy's chair.

"I just wanted to thank you personally," he said. "You may have saved our friendship."

"You're welcome," Nancy said. "But I'm sorry about your house."

"Yes, that was a tragedy," Mr. Bell said. "But there is good news—*my* insurance was paid. I'm going to build a new house on the exact same spot. I asked Mary to help me with the plans."

"And I said I would," Mrs. McGregor added, leaning over Nancy's other shoulder.

The two said good night and crossed the room arm in arm just as Cami pulled the string to release the purple and silver balloons. They floated gently down on the center of the room, surrounding Mr. Bell and Mrs. McGregor.

"It looks like a wedding," Bess said excitedly, watching the colorful display. "And Mr. Bell called her 'my Mary'! I bet they *will* get married and live happily ever after—and it's all thanks to you, Nancy Drew."

Nancy smiled to herself. She hoped Bess was right. She saw Mr. Bell pick up one of the balloons and present it to Mrs. McGregor as though it were a bouquet of flowers. The two elderly friends certainly did look very happy together.